Praise for
LILY DALE
AWAKENING

A Teenreads.com Best Book

"Readers will find this novel difficult to put down and will look forward to the second installment." —Teenreads.com

"This is a real page turner." —Bookdivas.com

"Characters are sharply drawn, and kids who like stories with psychic underpinnings will certainly appreciate the otherworldly goings-on and Calla's reactions to them." —*Booklist*

"Deft characterization couples with a compelling plot in a somewhat unique setting to create appeal particularly to young teens seeking meaning and agency in the face of life's difficulties." —*VOYA*

"If you love suspense, you'll love this book."
—Raven Gill, *VOYA* teen reviewer

BOOKS BY WENDY CORSI STAUB

THE LILY DALE SERIES:

AWAKENING

BELIEVING

CONNECTING

DISCOVERING

LILY DALE
AWAKENING

WENDY CORSI STAUB

Walker & Company
New York

First published in the United States of America in 2007 by
Walker Publishing Company, Inc.
Trade paperback edition published in 2008
Mass market edition published in 2009

Visit Walker & Company's Web site at www.walkeryoungreaders.com

For information about permission to reproduce selections from this book, write to
Permissions, Walker & Company, 175 Fifth Avenue, New York, New York 10010

The Library of Congress has cataloged the hardcover edition as follows:
Staub, Wendy Corsi.
Lily Dale : awakening / Wendy Corsi Staub.
p.   cm.
Summary: When seventeen-year-old Calla's mother suddenly dies, she goes to stay with
her psychic grandmother in Lily Dale, a spiritualist community in western New York,
where she discovers some disconcerting secrets about her practical, down-to-earth
mother, and realizes that she herself may also have some psychic abilities.
ISBN-13: 978-0-8027-9654-7 • ISBN-10: 0-8027-9654-0 (hardcover)
[1. Psychics—Fiction. 2. Psychic ability—Fiction. 3. Grandmothers—Fiction.
4. Mothers—Fiction. 5. New York (State)—Fiction. 6. Mystery and detective stories.]
I. Title.
PZ7.S804Li 2007   [Fic]—dc22   2007002370

ISBN-13: 978-0-8027-9843-5 • ISBN-10: 0-8027-9843-8 (mass market)

Typeset by Westchester Book Composition
Printed in the U.S.A. by Quebecor World Buffalo
2 4 6 8 10 9 7 5 3 1

All papers used by Walker & Company are natural, recyclable products made from
wood grown in well-managed forests. The manufacturing processes conform to the
environmental regulations of the country of origin.

Dedicated to my nieces and nephews, littlest to biggest:
Andrew Sypko, Dominick and Li'l Ricky Corsi, Leo James and
Hannah Rae Koellner, Caroline and Elizabeth Staub

And to Brody, Morgan, and Mark, my boys.

Written in loving memory of my mom, Francella Corsi

The author is grateful to agents Laura Blake Peterson and
Holly Frederick, as well as to Tracey Marchini, all at Curtis
Brown, Ltd.; to Nancy Berland, Elizabeth Middaugh, and staff
at Nancy Berland Public Relations; to Rick and Patty Dono-
van and Phil Pelleter at The Book Nook in Dunkirk, New
York; to Emily Easton and Deb Shapiro at Walker & Company; to David Ginsberg of Turnpike Entertainment; to Mark
and Morgan Staub for their literary expertise and creative
feedback; and to Brody Staub for pure sunshine and hugs.

PROLOGUE

Seventeen years ago

"Breathe, Stephanie. And focus on the lilacs, like they taught you in class. Come on . . ."

"They're . . . not . . . freaking . . . *lilacs* . . . Jeff," Stephanie pants to her husband, straining forward with the exertion. "They're . . . *lilies*."

Calla lilies, to be precise, but she's in too much pain to utter an extra word. And if she had enough energy to get one more out, it sure wouldn't be "calla."

No, it wouldn't be pretty.

"Are you sure?" Jeff is asking above her.

If she had the strength, she would probably reach out and jab him. Hard. This whole baby thing is his fault. If it weren't for him—

"Stephanie, sweetheart, don't forget to breathe."

1

It takes a moment for Stephanie to recognize the new voice, coming from somewhere near the bed. Odelia Lauder isn't prone to quiet, soothing inflection.

Stephanie's mother is more likely to jabber on and on in her usual excitable, opinionated way . . . unless she's giving a reading.

She's always quiet and soothing toward the strangers who come to her door day after day.

"Breathe, Stephanie. Breathe."

They don't always get along—all right, they rarely do—but Stephanie's glad she's here. Purely for her mother's sake, of course, she tells herself—Odelia would have been upset if she missed the chance to welcome her first grandchild.

But you need her here, too. You're in pain and you're afraid and you've already gone through hell—and she's the only one who knows about that. Just her and—

A tremendous contraction nearly tears her in two. *Oh, God. . . .*

She might be twenty-three years old, but she desperately needs her mommy. Needs to see her. She strains to get a glimpse of the familiar face.

"Mom!" she exclaims as her mother comes into view at last.

For God's sake, Mom, blue eye shadow?

That's what she wants to say, but she doesn't. Mostly because she can't.

All she can manage is, "When—?" before she's forced to break off, unable to push another word past the pain.

"I caught the first flight out of Buffalo this morning, and I had to change planes in Charlotte, and . . ."

Mom rambles on about her spur-of-the-moment trip to Florida, oblivious to the fact that another brutal contraction is sweeping in, until Stephanie screams in agony.

Then she says, again, calmly, "Breathe, Stephanie."

"Dammit! I'm . . . breathing . . . ," she bites out as the midwife bustles at the foot of the bed.

"Not the right way," Jeff reminds her. He gives an example of the rhythmic panting they learned in a childbirth prep class a few months ago.

So now she can't even breathe right?

Well, they're the wrong damned lilies. So there!

She'd say that aloud, but her abdomen is currently being crushed in an invisible vise.

They were supposed to be lilies of the valley, dammit!

She craves the delicate white blooms that grow wild in the woods near Lily Dale every spring; never tires of their heady scent. They have special meaning for her.

But nobody here, not even Mom, knows about that.

Anyway, a vase filled with lilies of the valley was supposed to be her focal point for labor, a technique suggested by the woman who taught the childbirth class at the hospital.

That was back when Jeff was still trying to convince her that a home birth attended by a midwife was dangerous. He couldn't understand why she was so reluctant to go to a hospital . . . and she couldn't tell him the truth.

The hospital might require too much information about her . . . past.

When Odelia visited from western New York, she took it upon herself to find a midwife and bring her over to meet

Stephanie, all in the space of a day. Ordinarily, Stephanie would have resented her mother's meddling. This time, she welcomed it.

Jeff was effectively overruled. It would be a home birth.

Still, Stephanie agreed that some of what they learned in the hospital class was useful.

Like the breathing.

And using a visual focal point.

But instead of her chosen lilies of the valley, the bedside table holds a stupid water glass filled with stupid supermarket-bought calla lilies. They were the best Jeff was able to do on short notice.

"They're white lilies," he said cluelessly when she told him they were all wrong. "You said white lilies."

She probably shouldn't have cursed him out, regardless of her excruciating pain. He was only trying to help, almost as nervous about becoming a father as she is about giving birth—even though *she* at least knows intuitively that everything will be all right.

She and the baby will both survive, and the baby will be a girl, regardless of the so-called penis the doctor saw on the ultrasound screen back in December.

Stephanie is no doctor, but that was no penis. It was the umbilical cord, or a shadow.

Her baby is a girl.

She knows that with absolute conviction, the way she's always known certain things.

Odelia doesn't realize her daughter shares that gift, though. And, of course, Jeff doesn't know about any of it. There are some facts—hugely important facts—he doesn't know about her past. And he never will, as far as she's concerned. He would never understand any of it. Look at Stephanie's father. He didn't get it . . . and he couldn't live with it . . . so he left.

If Jeff ever left . . .

Don't even think about that.

She's loved him from the moment they met. He's solid, stable, practical, reliable—everything she'd hoped for in a husband. Everything she never had, growing up with an eccentric mother and an absent father.

So she can't share everything with him. So what?

Everyone has secrets. Some more profound than others.

Their baby's gender has been an amusing secret for her to keep, considering how her husband has already bought a miniature Tampa Bay Buccaneers jersey for his "son," whom he plans to call Robert.

They haven't discussed girl names, and "Robert" is clearly out, so that little detail will have to be left until the last minute, which is a little frustrating.

Far more frustrating is the fact that Stephanie can't ever choose which information she receives.

It would have been most helpful if she knew that her water was going to break last night, a full month before her due date, in the middle of a crowded aisle at Publix.

She wasn't supposed to go into labor until mid-May. Which is why her mother was going to bring a bouquet of freshly picked lilies of the valley with her on the plane down from western New York.

But everything went wrong.

The baby is coming early, and the lilies of the valley aren't yet in bloom back home, and God knows you can't find them anywhere in Tampa on a moment's notice, even if you know what you're looking for, which Jeff apparently didn't, and—

"Oh, no!" Stephanie cries out as another wave of brutal pain radiates through her swollen body.

There's a flurry of activity around the foot of the bed.

The next thing she knows, Jeff and her mother have changed their "breathe" mantra to "push," counting their way to ten relentlessly every time they say it.

"Steph! Steph, he's here!" she hears Jeff announce as if from a great distance.

Then . . . "Wait a minute . . . He's a girl!"

She's vaguely conscious of laughter, of residual pain, of a baby's first cries. *Her* baby's first cries.

As she drifts off to blessed pain-free oblivion, she remembers something she heard back home in Lily Dale, years ago.

We cry coming into the world, as everyone around us laughs with joy. And we laugh with joy leaving the world, when everyone around us cries.

Stephanie is too out of it, and Jeff too wrapped up in his newborn daughter, for either of them to hear the quiet, meaningful exchange between Odelia and the midwife.

"There was a membrane over the baby's face, Odelia. Did you see?"

"A caul. Yes, I saw."

"You didn't look surprised."

"No. My mother said she was born with a caul, and so was I."

"What about Stephanie?"

6

"I had her in a hospital. I was unconscious. They gave you drugs back then. So I didn't see her."

"You do know what it means?"

"Yes," Odelia says thoughtfully, gazing over at the newborn child, snuggled in her unsuspecting father's embrace. "I know exactly what it means. But *he* doesn't. And if Stephanie has her way, I doubt my granddaughter ever will, either."

ONE

The Present

Here are the random thoughts that run through Calla Delaney's numb brain as she stands tearfully at her mother's bur-
ial service, flanked by her father and grandmother:

What if I faint?

What if I throw up?

*What if I lose it and start screaming or crying hysterically and
they have to carry me away?*

Oh, and *What is Kevin doing here?*

She can feel him here, even if she can't see him. But he's
not over there to the left with his parents and his younger sister, Lisa, who happens to be Calla's best bud since kindergarten.
Lisa grabbed her hand and squeezed it, hard, as Calla passed by
on her way from the limo, numbly following the white coffin
toward the gaping black hole waiting to swallow it.

Yes, loyal Lisa is here, crying her heart out in a stylish black dress with spaghetti straps, a wide-brimmed black straw hat, and spectator pumps. Even in mourning, she looks as though she just stepped off a mannequin's platform at Neiman Marcus.

Kevin, Calla senses, is somewhere toward the back of the crowd of mourners, symbolically banished from the front lines now that he and Calla are no longer a couple.

It's been over three months since he dumped her. When he did, Calla was positive that it was the worst thing that would ever happen to her, knew without a doubt that she had reached the rock-bottom depths of agony.

She was wrong.

God, she was so, so wrong.

"And so the soul of Stephanie Delaney is released from the body, and the body shall now be committed to the earth. . . ."

The minister—who is he, anyway?—sways back and forth as he speaks, sweat streaming over his fat red face, an open book in his hands.

Which book? Is it the Bible? A prayer book? An all-purpose funeral guide?

Calla wouldn't know. She and her parents don't go to church. It's not something she ever really thought much about, and definitely never with any measure of regret.

Never until now, anyway.

Now, she thinks of Lisa's—and Kevin's—Southern Baptist family. Lisa prays for everything from her grandfather being cured of cancer to David Connor finally asking her out. Neither of those things has happened yet, but Lisa hasn't given up. She just keeps on praying, certain that God will grant her wishes.

All the prayers in the world can't bring Mom back, Calla reminds herself, twisting her mother's emerald bracelet around and around on her wrist.

So in the end, what does it matter? Calla could have gone to church every day of her life, and she'd still be here, standing at her mother's grave in the wilting humidity of Florida in July. Helpless. Angry. Distraught.

I can't take much more of this. If this isn't over soon, I'm going to . . .

I don't know what. Just lose it.

Oh, Mom . . .

She closes her eyes, hard, and tears roll freely down her cheeks once again, leaving a hot, stinging trail like toxic rain.

What am I going to do without you?

Calla loves her father, of course . . . but how can it be just the two of them from here on in? They're rarely, if ever, alone together.

Now that's all they'll ever be.

What will they do? Or eat? Or say?

It would be easier, Calla thinks irrationally, if her grandmother lived closer.

Never mind that Odelia Lauder, with her rotund figure, dyed-red curls, purple nail polish and matching strands of beads, is a classic whack job—according to pragmatic Mom, anyway.

But at least if Odelia were around, things wouldn't be so—

Her grandmother abruptly reaches for Calla's hand and clasps it tightly.

Almost as if she's just read Calla's mind.

11

Which is interesting considering that she's seen Odelia Lauder exactly twice in the past decade, both brief and awkward encounters at family funerals up north.

Of course, before Mom and Grandma had their final falling out in a highly charged scene Calla dimly recalls from her early childhood, Odelia was a regular fixture in their lives.

She's always lived back in western New York, in Lily Dale, Mom's tiny hometown. Calla has never been there. When Calla grew old enough to ask her mother why, she said it was because of the weather.

"It's always cold and unpredictable and stormy. They get feet and feet of snow."

"Always?" Calla asked dubiously. "What about summer? Why can't we go visit then?"

Her mother never had a satisfactory answer for that question.

Odelia used to visit them in Tampa, though. Calla vaguely remembers sitting on her lap reading stories, stringing clay beads, singing funny little songs. But the memories are surreal, almost as if they happened to somebody else.

Kind of like this, today. The funeral.

If only it *were* happening to somebody else.

Tears spill past the frames of her sunglasses and trickle down her cheeks.

It's so hot. Everything is ominously still, the sky oppressive. It's going to storm.

Calla shifts her weight, slips her hand out of her grandmother's to reach into the pocket of her black skirt for a fresh tissue. Her mother's black skirt, actually. This is Mom's suit, one she wears—*wore*—to her bank job, a well-cut designer crepe in a size 6. Not exactly Calla's style, but why would she ever own a black suit in the first place? Unlike Lisa, she's usually in shorts and T-shirts.

Anyway, it fits perfectly. She and her mother have—*had*—the same long legs, long waist, slim build.

"You look so much like her, Calla. . . ."

How many times has she heard that phrase in these past forty-eight hours?

Not that she hasn't been hearing it her entire life. Like her mother, she has thick milk-chocolate-colored hair with streaks of lighter brown; wide-set hazel eyes that go green or gray, depending on the day; even a faint patch of freckles on the bridge of her smallish—for her face, anyway—nose.

She looks nothing like her father, who has pitch-black hair and blacker eyes.

Sometimes Dad laughs when people ask if she's the mailman's kid. Sometimes he doesn't. Especially when the person who's saying it is a guy who's flirting with Mom.

Flirting.

That makes her think of Kevin. She turns her head, slightly, seeking that familiar sun-streaked mop of hair, those big blue eyes fastened to her from wherever it is that he's standing.

She does see big blue eyes, filled with tears.

But they belong to his sister, and Lisa isn't looking at Calla. She's staring, in sorrowful horror, at the coffin and the grave.

Calla can feel Kevin—or someone else?—watching her intently. The sensation is as palpable as the rolling rumble of thunder in the distance.

She turns again slightly and scans the crowd. There are a

bunch of kids here from Shoreside Day School. Like Tiffany Foxwood, who—on the last day of school back in May—snickered when Calla tripped over Nick Rodriguez's sprawled legs in the cafeteria, almost sending her chef salad flying.

Nick didn't trip her on purpose. In fact, he said, "Whoa, good save, Delaney."

But Tiffany, notoriously bitchy, snickered. Right, and here she is now, staring blatantly as if taking notes to report back to her coven. *Yeah, you should have seen Calla, she was a mess, no makeup whatsoever, her face was all raw and she never stopped crying, not once. Oh, and she was the one who found her mother, you know. And she didn't even check for a pulse. She ran screaming into the street like a raving lunatic, and the old guy next door, the one who's almost deaf, actually heard her and called 911.*

The old guy next door is here, too, Mr. Evans, along with a group of elderly neighbors, no strangers to loss themselves at their age. And there are a few teachers from Shoreside: Mr. Hayes and Ms. Valvo and Mrs. Durkin. Dozens of Mom's coworkers from the bank are here, and a bunch of faculty from the college where Dad is a professor.

Calla turns her head again, this time a little farther, still looking for *him*.

The piercing scrutiny boring into her from behind, somewhere to the right, might just as well be a hand on her shoulder, so strong is the presence. This, she knows on a gut level, is different from the stares of her classmates who came to the funeral home last night, some out of genuine sympathy, others, she knows, out of mere morbid curiosity.

It has to be Kevin. Who else can it be? Who else would be focused solely on Calla?

"Ashes to ashes, dust to dust. . . ." The minister is spewing cliches—okay, so maybe they're prayers—seemingly oblivious as the thunder grows closer and lightning slashes the purple-black summer sky, low, beyond the cemetery.

The storm is coming right at them, off the distant Gulf. Calla fights the potent urge to flee—not just the storm, but all of it, the minister, the heat, the coffin, the grave—even as a stronger, more pressing urge takes hold.

She gives in to that one swiftly, swiveling her neck around completely to the right, not caring that it's probably impolite to turn your head at a funeral.

Nope. No Kevin there.

But she immediately spots the person who's been watching her.

To her surprise, it's a total stranger.

The woman, clad in a flowing white dress, is standing apart from the black-clad crowd of mourners. Just a few feet, but enough of a gap to make Calla wonder why she isn't standing with everybody else. She isn't way over there under the cluster of palm trees for the shade, because there's no sun; she isn't there for shelter from the rain, because it has yet to start falling.

She stands in stark isolation, black hair pulled back into a bun, eyes so darkly intense that Calla feels goose bumps rising on her arms as she meets the woman's gaze.

It isn't that her expression is unkind . . .

More that it's just . . . odd.

Oddly focused only on Calla, in the midst of Stephanie's bereaved husband and mother, friends and colleagues.

Why is she staring at me?

Who is she?

And why is she wearing white at a funeral?

A sudden clap of thunder followed by a frighteningly close flash of lightning startles Calla into turning her head away from the strange woman.

The minister's words grow rushed; the crowd stirs uneasily.

Still unsettled by the stranger's stare, Calla turns to look for the woman again.

The spot beneath the stand of palm trees is empty, as is the grass around it.

A quick scan shows that the woman didn't join the crowd of mourners, and she's not hurrying toward a waiting car to escape the rain.

She's simply gone.

But . . . how can that be? People don't just disappear into thin air.

She had to be a figment of my imagination in the first place, Calla tells herself uneasily.

What other explanation is there?

The storm has blown in full force, drawing the service to a hasty close.

The coffin has been lowered into the waiting vault, now pooled with rainwater.

"Let's go, honey," Odelia says from beneath a black umbrella. Somebody must have handed it to her, because she isn't the type to carry one—that would mean planning ahead—and even if she were, it certainly wouldn't be black. Electric orange, maybe. Or neon green. Or polka dots.

For a moment, Calla forgets to be grief stricken.

Then she glances at her father and remembers.

She watches him being tearfully embraced by his only brother, her uncle Scott, who lives in Chicago.

"Calla."

She looks up at the sound of a familiar voice. There he is. *Kevin.*

Gone are the sun-streaked surfer-boy locks he used to have. His blond hair is stubble short and he's wearing a dark suit with a white shirt and black tie. She's seen him dressed up on only two occasions, at the prom and at his graduation. But that was over a year ago. He's changed. He looks older. Almost like a man now.

"Hey," he says softly.

She opens her mouth but can't find her voice.

"Are you okay?"

She just stares mutely at him. Is she *okay*? Is he freaking kidding her?

"I'm so sorry, about your mom, and . . . about . . . everything." He reaches out and wraps his fingers around her upper arm.

She desperately wants to pull away from him, but she can't.

She won't, because his touch is warm, familiar—and right now, nothing else is.

"Is there anything I can do?"

She shakes her head.

"Are you . . . is it that you can't talk, or that you won't? I mean, to me?"

She clears her throat, manages to say, "It's not you. I'm upset, okay? Obviously. And not about you. Okay?"

She expects him to release his hold on her arm, but he doesn't.

"Calla . . . look, I still care about you. I said I wanted us to be friends and I meant it."

"No you didn't. Not then."

You only mean it now because you're feeling guilty.

At last, she finds the strength to pull her arm from his grasp. His hand lingers in the air, making him seem helpless. Less like a man, more like a little boy who doesn't quite know what to do with himself.

He hesitates. "Listen, if you need . . ." He pauses, and she expects him to say *me.*

But he doesn't. He says *anything.*

"If you need anything, I'm around."

She shrugs. She wants to tell him that she doesn't need anything. Not from him.

But it would be a lie. And if there's anything her mother taught her, it was never to lie.

Calla watches Kevin walk away, hands in his pockets and head bowed, to join his parents and Lisa. They get into their white Lexus and drive away. Mrs. Wilson is sitting in the back with Lisa, her arms wrapped around her, comforting her.

For a moment, Calla is so insanely jealous that she feels physically sick.

She wants to be Lisa, wrapped in her mother's arms.

No, she doesn't.

She wants to be Calla, wrapped in her own mother's arms.

She blinks away tears, steps closer to her father, and stares at her mother's grave.

A shadow falls over the ground in front of her, and she looks up to see a man in sunglasses and a dark suit passing by. His head is bowed in sorrow, and she can't tell who he is. Just another person who's mourning Mom. Calla never realized just how many people Stephanie Delaney touched in her life, until she saw the crowd here today.

"So let me know if you want her to come stay," Uncle Scott is telling Dad as Calla listens idly, her insides twisting in agony. She still feels sick.

What if I throw up?

She supposes it really doesn't matter now. People have dispersed quickly, running through the rain to their cars.

The cool droplets feel good. . . .

But we shouldn't be hanging around out here with lightning splitting the sky.

Then again, what does it matter? If she's struck by lightning, she'll be with Mom again.

The man passing by the grave raises his dark glasses to his forehead and looks up at the sky. Catching a better glimpse of his face, Calla recognizes him . . . sort of.

Who is he, exactly?

Oh. He's one of Mom's coworkers or something. Right. She met him when he stopped by the house one day not long ago to give something to Mom, and Calla answered the door.

His name was Todd. Or Tom. Something like that. She watches dully as he walks away toward the thinning line of cars parked at the edge of the cemetery.

Her father, looking as out of place in his dark suit as Calla feels in hers, removes his wire-rimmed glasses to dab away the tears that seem to just keep coming. "I don't know, Scott . . . ," he's saying. "That would be such an imposition and you guys already have a full house."

"There's always room for one more. She can bunk with the girls and help Susie out around the house. She could really use a hand. And you know how the kids love Calla."

What?

Talk about a lightning bolt. . . .

They're discussing *her?*

No. No way.

No way is Calla moving in with her aunt and uncle and their four kids, all under seven years old.

Has her father lost his mind?

Or . . .

Hurt washes over her.

Is he so reluctant to be a single dad that he's shipping her off to another family?

Numb, she opens her mouth to protest, but she can't seem to find her voice.

"What do you think, kiddo?" Uncle Scott asks, turning to Calla as a hard lump swells in her throat. "How would you like to spend the rest of the summer in Chicago?"

Just the rest of the summer?

Oh.

Just the rest of the summer.

Okay, but still . . .

"We're going to California in August," she reminds her father.

He's about to start a two-semester sabbatical in the physics department at Shellborne College. At least . . . that *was* the plan.

Mom, a total workaholic, had even reluctantly arranged to take a few weeks of saved vacation so that she and Calla could spend the remainder of the summer out west with Dad before Calla began her senior year at Shoreside Day in Tampa. Of course, Mom was torn about going away for so long. She kept asking how her office was going to get along without her. Dad's retort was the same every time: "Well, how am *I* supposed to get along without you?"

How bittersweet those words are now.

"Calla—" Her father breaks off, looking overwhelmed.

"You rented that place for us near the beach for the month of August," Calla tells him. Then, seeing the look on his face, she adds in a small voice, "Didn't you?"

"I did, yes . . . when you and your mom were going to come out with me. But without her . . . it's expensive, Calla. Really expensive. More than we can afford . . . now."

"Where are we going to stay, then?" She doesn't dare allow herself to consider the larger question: *What's going to happen when it's time for me to go back to Tampa and start school?*

"You and your dad need to talk," Uncle Scott tells her.

"We just . . . we have a lot to figure out," Dad says, more to Uncle Scott than to her. "It doesn't have to be today, or even tomorrow."

"There isn't much time, Jeff. You have to make a decision."

"No, I know. I just can't think straight."

Calla walks away, her heart pounding. So Dad doesn't want her to go to California with him now? He'd rather send her off to be Aunt Susie's summer slave? The cousins are brats, the house is a crumb-and-cat-fur-filled wreck, and where the heck would Calla "bunk," as her uncle so charmingly put it, in his daughters' tiny, toy-clogged room?

And what about September? What then?

Miserable, she crouches beside her mother's grave as fat raindrops plop into the sandy soil heaped beside it. She reaches blindly for a handful and sprinkles it over the wet white coffin.

"Good-bye, Mommy," she whispers.

At that moment, the loose clasp on the emerald bracelet releases.

Calla gasps, helplessly watching as it falls into the gaping hole, like it's determined to go with its rightful owner.

She and her mother had a fight not long ago about Calla's borrowing the coveted bracelet without asking. Mom said the clasp was loose and she was bound to lose it. Then Kevin broke up with her, and Mom, feeling sorry for her, gave her the bracelet.

"It's yours to keep," she said, hugging Calla. "I know it's just jewelry. It won't heal a broken heart, but it might make you feel better for a couple of minutes."

It did.

Now, Calla searches for the bracelet in the shadowed depths of the grave.

"Come on, honey." Her father is behind her, tugging her arm. "Get up. Let's go."

"But . . ."

"Calla, she isn't in there. Not really. Don't you remember what we talked about when we saw her at the funeral home?"

Yes. Of course she remembers.

She'll never forget the macabre sight of her mother's corpse in the open casket . . . or the startlingly cold, unyielding feel of her flesh beneath Calla's lips when she kissed her good-bye one last time before they closed the lid.

"You have to let go now, honey," her father says. "Come on."

"I know, but . . . my bracelet."

"What?" her father asks, and his voice is choked with grief, his face ravaged by it.

"Never mind," Calla says softly, taking his hand as they walk through the falling rain toward the waiting limo.

TWO

"This is absolutely crazy," Jeff Delaney mutters, pacing a short distance through the crowded gate area to check the Departures screen for the third time in as many minutes.

"Dad, planes are delayed all the time," Calla reminds him, scrolling through the playlist on her iPod again as he plops restlessly beside her. "And it's only by a half hour, which is actually not all *that* crazy. I've heard of people being stuck in airports for—"

"No, not the delay. I mean . . . *this*." He waves his hand in her general direction.

"*I'm* crazy?"

"No, *I'm* crazy for sending you a thousand miles away for so long."

"It's only for a couple of weeks, really." Three, to be exact. By Labor Day, Calla will join him out west as the new kid in some school she's never even heard of.

A short time ago, that would have been a fate worse than . . .

No. No fate is worse than what she's just been through. She knows that now.

"What was I thinking?" Dad shakes his head.

"You were thinking logically," she assures him, tucking the iPod into her pocket. "You were thinking that I can't come with you now because you'll be too busy getting settled, and there's nowhere for me to even stay with you."

The beach house is history. He'll sleep on a friend's pull-out couch in a cramped condo until he finds an affordable place to rent in a good school district starting in September. Public school—not private, like Shoreside. He seems much more worried about money now than he did before Mom died. Calla figures their finances are pretty dire without Mom's salary or even a life insurance policy. She overheard Dad say that Mom didn't have one. When Calla asked about money, he said they'll be fine, that they'll have more than enough. Somehow, she doubts that.

He needs a haircut, Calla notices as she watches him rake a hand through his shaggy black hair. That was Mom's department—along with his wardrobe. She had planned to go shopping to buy him some decent clothes for the sabbatical. She wanted him to get contact lenses, too. She thought the glasses made him look too "professorish," as she said.

"I *am* a professor," Dad protested, more than once . . . because she said it pretty frequently.

Mom is—*was*—big on appearances. That was why she talked Dad into moving, a few years back, from their bunga-low in the historic district to a nice new home off Westshore.

Dad said they couldn't afford it. Mom said they could. She won that argument. She usually did.

Not that she had to have the most expensive designer clothes or extravagant jewelry, but she liked to be well put together, and she expected Calla and her father to follow suit.

Which was fine—at least, for Calla. Why argue with a mother who enjoyed taking you shopping for hours on end?

But Dad . . . well, he was the kind of man who would—and once did—absentmindedly walk out the front door wearing only boxer shorts.

He still *is* that kind of man, Calla reminds herself now.

Dad = present tense; Mom = past. You'd think that after a few weeks, she'd have her tenses straight.

Yeah, well, this isn't an English test. It's Calla's life, sad as it is. A life that's about to take yet another dramatic turn. At least this is one she instigated herself. With a little help from her grandmother. Which is where the "crazy" part comes in.

But her only alternatives to Lily Dale are Chicago—*no way*—or staying here in Florida with Lisa's family—also *no way*. They offered, and Lisa did her best to talk Calla into it, but . . .

Well, Lisa's parents are Kevin's parents. Lisa's house is Kevin's house, and he's still home for the summer. What if he decides to bring his new girlfriend home to meet his parents?

He does have one. He wouldn't admit it when they broke up, and Lisa swears he hasn't mentioned anybody, but Calla *knows*, the way she just *knows* she's meant to go to Lily Dale.

It was Odelia's idea. And when her grandmother first brought it up before she left Tampa after the funeral, Calla decided she really *is* a whack job.

Then Jeff, without even hesitating for a split second,

adamantly said no way. At which point Calla found herself deciding it might not be such a bad idea after all.

She couldn't help it. Dad, who used to be such a nonissue in her life, has been bugging her. Mom was the one who used to fill that role—and who was also the one she confided in, the one whose time and attention Calla craved. Probably because she was always so busy with work. Calla missed her when she was away at banking conferences—which was more and more often this past year—and part of the reason Dad had insisted she take some time off.

Calla feels guilty now admitting, even to herself, that as much as she missed her mother when she was gone, she also appreciated the break from the household tension. Her parents argued a lot lately, and so did Calla and her mother.

Calla might look like Mom, but she's always acted more like her father. They're both quiet and a little absentminded, both can get caught up in something—like reading a book or listening to music or surfing the Internet—only to realize they've wasted away an entire day. That sort of unproductive behavior drove Mom crazy, and it was the source of some frustrating, no-win arguments around their household.

Life would probably be a lot easier for Calla if she had her mother's super-efficiency and organizational skills, her practicality, and above all, her supreme confidence. Calla sometimes has a hard time thinking of things to say to people.

Especially guys.

Guys who aren't Kevin, anyway. Kevin she's known since kindergarten, so she never thought of him as a "guy." He was just Lisa's brother . . . until the day he suddenly noticed her during sophomore year.

She saw it happen. She and Lisa were in the Wilsons' pool, and Kevin came out of the house, jangling car keys, just as Calla climbed onto the diving board. He more or less stopped short, and she could feel his eyes on her in a way they had never been before.

He tossed aside the keys and hung around by the pool with Calla and Lisa instead—a first. And he offered to give Calla a ride home that night, courtesy of his newly obtained driver's license. She could feel the vibe between them as they drove through the darkened streets of Tampa, not saying much, listening to Alicia Keys.

When he pulled up in front of her house, she thanked him and started to climb out of the car. He reached past her, pulled the door closed so that the interior light went off again, took her into his arms, and kissed her.

That was the beginning. After two great years, last spring was the end. But not the worst *end* that can happen to a person.

Oh, Mom. I can't believe I'll never see you again.

Never again will she look at her mother and feel as though she's seeing herself a couple of decades in the future; never again will they stand back to back, laughing, as Calla's father checks to see who is taller. It's been a draw at five foot seven since Calla was a freshman.

I was supposed to grow taller than you. It was going to happen any day now. You said it yourself. You said you had one last growth spurt when you were my age.

You never said you were going to die, dammit! How could you leave me?

"Are you okay?" Dad asks anxiously, and she looks up to see him watching her.

"I'm fine." She flashes a bright, fake smile.

She *has* to be fine. She can't go with him to California. She can't stay at the Wilsons with Kevin home for a few more weeks. She *won't* go to Chicago with Uncle Scott and Aunt Susie.

That leaves Odelia and Lily Dale. Case closed.

Look at the bright side. There probably aren't a whole lot of rules in Odelia's house.

That isn't based on intuition, it's based on common sense. Anybody who eats gummy worms for breakfast and cold hot dogs, straight from the package, for a midnight snack—both of which Odelia did while she was staying with them— probably isn't a stickler for rules.

Mom had a lot of rules; rules Dad didn't bother to enforce whenever she was away on business. He was just . . . well, *there.* She loved him, but she never paid much attention to him, and vice versa.

Now he's all she has, and she's all he has, and . . . well, he's kind of driving her crazy. He's grown much more strict since Mom died. He's barely let Calla out of his sight, almost as if he thinks that if he can't see her, something awful might happen to her, too.

She looks down at her plane ticket to Buffalo with a sudden stab of regret.

Less than an hour from now, she'll be at thirty-five thousand feet, winging her way more than a thousand miles away from her dad. Not long after she gets on her plane, he'll return to the airport with his luggage to get on his, which will take him to the West Coast.

The sudden ringing of her cell phone in her pocket is a welcome distraction. "Hello?"

"I miss you already."

Lisa. Calla smiles wistfully. "I miss you already, too."

"Then don't go! Come here."

"You know I can't do that," she says, casting a glance at her father, who appears to be lost in thought. "And you know why."

"He's going back to school in a few weeks. You can avoid each other till then."

"Under the same roof? I doubt it."

"Who knows? Maybe if you come here, you'll get back together," Lisa says, and Calla's heart—oblivious to things like logic or likelihood—soars.

"That's not going to happen," she tells Lisa resolutely.

"I honestly think he still loves you."

"He has a funny way of showing it," she says bitterly, remembering the shocking text message he sent back in April. He couldn't even wait to dump her in person. It was too urgent to put on hold until his spring semester at Cornell drew to a close; it required immediate action via cell phone. "Look, Lisa, I've got to go. My flight is boarding."

Seeing her father look up at that statement, she realizes he's been eavesdropping. Well, he can hardly help it, sitting right beside her. Still, it bugs her. Even though she knows he's probably wondering what happened between her and Kevin. Comforting her through the breakup was Mom's department. Dad never even acknowledged it—before or after Mom died. Maybe it was too awkward a topic for him. Or maybe he was just too caught up in his own grief that he didn't consider her recently broken heart. Or maybe he is glad that as a newly single parent, he doesn't have to deal with a college-aged boyfriend.

She promises Lisa she'll call or IM her later, hangs up, and sighs.

"Lisa?" Dad asks. As if he didn't know. "It's not too late to change your mind and stay."

"I don't want to do that."

"I just wish there were somewhere else you could go. Or *would* go," Dad adds, obviously thinking of Uncle Scott.

"Well, there isn't."

"Yeah. I know," he says flatly—and sadly. He's probably thinking of his parents now.

Dad's mother, Calla's Nana Norma, died a few years ago, and his father, Calla's Poppy Ted, lives in a nursing home not far from Uncle Scott. He has Alzheimer's. When Nana died, Calla's father and Uncle Scott went together to tell him. He sobbed inconsolably. He even went to the funeral. The next day, he asked Dad why Norma hadn't paid her daily visit. Dad was forced to break the news all over again that she had died. Poppy sobbed inconsolably. And the next day, he woke up looking for her again.

Poor Poppy. Now that Calla understands the profound shock and grief of losing the person closest to you, she can't imagine having to wake up and relive it every single day for the rest of her life.

"Dad, for what it's worth, I'm glad I'm going to Lily Dale," Calla feels obligated to assure him—or maybe both of them—yet again. "It'll help me to feel closer to Mom."

"Calla . . ." He stops, as though he has no idea what he wants to say.

"Dad, I need to see where Mom—"

"Calla, she left home when she was your age and never

31

went back. She didn't even like to talk about it, so I don't know how—"

"Lily Dale was her life for eighteen years," she cuts in. "Maybe she didn't talk about it much, but she wasn't big on reminiscing. You know that."

He nods. Of course he knows that. Mom was all about the here and now. She never wanted to look back, and she never wanted to look ahead.

"Let's just be," she used to say. "I don't like remember-whens or what-ifs, and I don't like plans."

"Lily Dale used to be her home," Calla tells her dad gently, noticing that he's once again wearing the now-familiar expression he gets when he's about to cry. "It was home to Mom the way Tampa is home to me."

Not that it feels like home anymore, she thinks glumly.

Everything has changed. Mom's gone, school's out, Kevin's no longer in her life. Even her friendship with Lisa is different. Calla can hardly pop in and out of her friend's house the way she used to—not when she'd risk running into Kevin there. Lisa comes over to the Delaneys' when Calla asks, but she can tell her friend is uncomfortable there now. Spooked, almost. Whenever she walks in the front door, she glances nervously at the spot at the foot of the stairs where Stephanie died.

Calla herself goes out of her way to avoid it, which means getting out of the house whenever possible. It isn't easy to escape her father's watchful eye, but every time he's otherwise occupied, she's out of there.

She's spent a lot of time these past few weeks wandering aimlessly along the winding streets of her development, gazing longingly at the houses occupied by people whose lives haven't been shattered. Every glimpse of strangers going about their daily business brings a pang: the retiree pruning her gardenias, the businessman checking his mailbox, the little girls practicing cartwheels on the grass.

Shocking, to Calla, that the rest of the world is still carrying on as usual.

She'll be glad to get away from Tampa, even though she's about to spend three weeks in a strange place with a virtual stranger who's—well, not to be mean to Odelia, but she's . . . *strange*.

"Grandma!"

"Darling!"

Calla stops walking so that the girl behind her can rush past, straight into the arms of a little old lady waiting by the Arrivals gate. The woman has a white bun, glasses on a chain, and is wearing a double-knit pantsuit with sensible brown shoes.

After allowing herself a wistful glance at them, Calla looks around for Odelia, who doesn't have a white bun and wears her pink-rimmed cat's-eye glasses high in her dyed-red curls when they're not balanced on the tip of her nose.

She wouldn't be caught dead in double knit or sensible shoes. No, she's more likely to wear . . .

Birkenstocks and yellow capris.

That's exactly what she has on, and after spotting her, Calla debates—but only for a split second—fleeing before Odelia spots her.

You can't do that. It's not like there's anyplace else to go.

Sure there is. You can hop a flight to Europe. Or some island where you can start over and nobody will know who you are or what happened to you. You can—

"Calla! Yoo-hoo! Calla, here I am!"

Yes, there she is, running with open arms and the most welcoming smile ever.

"I'm so, so happy you made it. You don't know how thrilled I am to have you here."

In that moment, Calla senses with overwhelming clarity that she's right where she should be. "Hi," she says, her voice muffled by Odelia's generous cleavage.

"How was your flight? Were you afraid?"

"Afraid? No, I knew the flight would be okay."

Odelia smiles an odd little smile. "So did I."

Before Calla can contemplate the possible implication of that strange smile, Odelia says in a rush, "Let's get your luggage and blow this pop shop. I'm double-parked."

Calla smiles. Of course she is.

Less than ten minutes later, they're standing beside an ancient, beat-up cherry-red convertible.

"Um, do you want to pop the trunk so I can put my luggage in?" Calla asks, dragging her suitcase around to the back.

Odelia laughs. "This trunk doesn't *pop*. That invention's way before its time. I'm surprised there isn't a rumble seat in there someplace."

"A what?"

"Never mind. That's way before *your* time, too. Get in, and I'll take care of your bags."

Calla obediently climbs into the passenger's seat, then spots a white rectangle propped beneath the windshield wiper on the driver's side. "Uh-oh. You got a ticket," she calls.

"Oh, that? I got it years ago. Paid it, too."

"Then what—?"

"I carry it with me whenever I come to the airport. It's good for something. I just put it on the windshield, and the parking patrols leave me alone."

What is there to say except *Oh*.

Well, there's *Wow*.

There's other stuff, too. Far less tolerant than *Oh* or *Wow*. She can just imagine what her upstanding, law-abiding, sensible father would say about Odelia's all-purpose parking ticket.

Then again, Dad doesn't know any of this. *And he doesn't have to know*, Calla reminds herself. *I'm on my own now.* She just isn't sure she knows how to feel about that.

"Ready to go down to Lily Dale?" Odelia asks, getting into the driver's seat.

"Ready," Calla tells her. "How far is it?"

"You mean in miles, or time?"

"Time, I guess."

"About an hour if someone else were driving, but I can get us there faster."

"I'll bet," Calla murmurs, fastening her seat belt. She has a feeling she's going to need it.

The farther they get from the New York State Thruway exit, the more rural the scenery.

"We're really in the country," Calla notes, gazing out the open car window at a couple of black-and-white cows grazing in a pasture bordered by a grape vineyard.

"What did you say?" Odelia turns down the radio.

CD player, actually. She's singing along with an old Bob Dylan song on a homemade mix that includes Dylan, the Dead, the Band, and, inexplicably, the Red Hot Chili Peppers.

"Never mind," Calla tells her, figuring her grandmother knows she lives in the country. It's just news to Calla, who pictured a small upstate New York town as being more, well, tourist-friendly. But she hasn't seen a restaurant or hotel for a few miles now.

Plus, Odelia described Lily Dale as a gated community. Calla is pretty familiar with those, considering that she lives in a nice one off Westshore back home. But she's having a hard time picturing an exclusive suburban development plunked out here in the middle of nowhere.

She shivers a little in the cool breeze blowing through the window, but she doesn't roll it up. You don't get to drive with your car windows down in Florida very often, and she likes the feeling of the wind in her hair.

Just when she's about to ask how much farther they have to go, Odelia brakes and screeches onto a side road. "We'll go this way," she says. "Less traffic."

Traffic? Calla wants to laugh but doesn't dare. It might be insulting to point out that the only "traffic" they've seen so far was a four-car backup caused by a slow-moving tractor.

They pass a number of houses, some of them more like cottages, really. Then they round a bend and a small blue lake comes into view. A lake?

There was something about a lake, she remembers suddenly. When her mother and grandmother had their emotional falling out that long-ago day, one of them said something about a lake. No, not *said—screamed.* They were both shrill,

Calla recalls, and crying. And when Odelia stormed out, her mother told her never to come back. She never did . . . until the funeral.

"What is that water?" Calla asks her grandmother, hoping to jog her memory.

"It's Cassadaga Lake. And over there is the Leolyn Hotel." Odelia indicates a large old building that doesn't look like any hotel Calla has ever seen. It looks more like a haunted house.

"Isn't there, like, a Marriott around here?" she asks, wondering where her father is going to stay if he visits.

Odelia laughs so hard she almost misses another turn. "Oops, here we are." Scrambling, she corrects her steering, which sends them careening through the old-fashioned wrought-iron entrance to Lily Dale. There's a guard—Odelia waves at him—but no actual gate.

Obviously, gated communities up north are nothing like they are in Tampa, Calla thinks, looking around. She's so busy gazing in dismay at the first smattering of small gingerbread structures, which must be over a hundred years old and look as though they haven't been touched since they were built, that she fails to notice the sign as they pass it.

Lily Dale Assembly . . . World's Largest Center for the Religion of Spiritualism

THREE

Odelia's home is a stone's throw from the main gate, on a tree-shaded lane called Cottage Row. The name fits. This small two-story structure is definitely more cottage than house, with its peeling pastel pinkish-orange paint and masses of flowers growing on either side of the front-porch steps.

The garden looks as though it were planted by someone who closed her eyes and threw handfuls of seeds at the soil—and it probably was, knowing Odelia's slapdash style.

Calla can't help but contrast these beds, overflowing with clashing blossoms of pink and orange, purple and red, with the ones her mother designed back home: carefully tended plots filled with mostly calming shades of white and cream, accented by lots of lush green tropical foliage. Of course, there were lots of Mom's all-time favorite lilies, the waxy cone-shaped blossoms for which Calla was named.

"Why do they call this place Lily Dale if there are no

lilies?" Calla asks after a quick glance around as they climb the steps, each of them hauling a heavy piece of Calla's luggage.

"Oh, there are lilies. Your mother's old favorites aren't in bloom now, but they're called lilies of the valley. They're little white bell-shaped blossoms the size of your pinky fingernail, but they give off a tremendous scent." Odelia's smile is sadly nostalgic. "When they pop up everywhere in late spring every year, I think of your mother . . . and of you."

"Of me? Why? I'm named after calla lilies." She's pretty sure those striking, elegant flowers don't grow just anywhere. Brides carry them in bouquets, fancy restaurants have them in vases, but you never stumble across a random patch of them.

"Well, your father made a mistake when your mother was having you," Odelia informs her. "Stephanie sent him out to get lilies of the valley when she went into labor, and he brought back calla lilies instead."

"You were there?" she asks, doubting it, and is surprised when Odelia nods. "And Mom didn't like calla lilies?" Calla tries not to take that personally.

"No, she *did*. In fact, they became her favorite, because of you. But when she was your age, living here, she was crazy about lilies of the valley. She loved the way they smelled."

Calla frowns, suddenly noticing an overpowering floral scent wafting in the air. She sniffs, looking around for the source and finding nothing.

"After Stephanie left Lily Dale," Odelia goes on, seemingly oblivious to the mysterious tide of fragrance, "I'd bring her lilies of the valley, and she'd say they reminded her of home."

Home? Oh. She's talking about *this* home, of course. Not

their house in Tampa, a three-thousand-square-foot contemporary with professional landscaping and a pool.

That this shabby little cottage in this shabby little town was ever home to her mother catches her by surprise all over again. Somehow, she forgot for a few minutes that this isn't just Odelia's home.

Calla sniffs the air again and is relieved to note that the floral scent has vanished just as abruptly as it materialized. Maybe it was her imagination; they were talking about flowers.

"Jacy! Come on over here and meet my granddaughter!" she hears Odelia call, and looks up in dismay. She isn't in the mood to meet—

A gorgeous guy her age?

With his glossy black hair, black eyes fringed by lush lashes, and olive complexion, he looks a little like Billy Pijuan, a friend of hers at Shoreline. Billy's Cuban. Maybe this guy is as well, with those exotic looks. He's tall and lanky, dressed casually in a gray T-shirt and shorts.

Calla's hand lifts to smooth her windblown hair as she glances down to make sure she didn't dribble Coke on the front of her white top on the plane. Nope, all clean.

"Calla, this is Jacy Bly. He lives across the way." Odelia points vaguely at the grassy green. "Jacy, this is my granddaughter, Calla—the one I was telling you about."

Uh-oh. What could Odelia have possibly told this guy about her?

"Nice to meet you," Calla says politely, and sticks out her right hand, the way her mother taught her to do whenever she's introduced to someone new.

"You, too." Soft-spoken Jacy grasps her hand, and Calla

nearly gasps. A current of—what, electricity?—seems to have shot up her right arm.

Okay, that's ridiculous. But she didn't imagine it. Her arm is still tingling as he releases her hand. Maybe it was static electricity or something?

She looks at Jacy to see if he seems jolted, but it's impossible to read anything on his beautiful, enigmatic face.

"Want to come in and have some lemonade with us, Jacy?"

"No, thanks," he tells Odelia. "I have to go."

Calla does her best not to turn her head and stare after him as he walks away. "He seems nice," she says casually to her grandmother, watching her open the door—which, Calla can't help but notice, wasn't even locked.

"He is nice. Come on in." Odelia holds the door for her.

Stepping over the threshold, Calla immediately sees a steep flight of stairs. Uh-oh. Instant flashback to what happened back home . . . to what she found there at the foot of the stairs when she walked in the front door that day after her social studies final.

Mom. Long brown hair tousled around her head, matted with clotting blood. Neck twisted. Eyes open. Vacant. Gone.

No, don't think about that. Just focus on where you are right now. The past is in the past.

She follows Odelia from the foyer into the next dim, cluttered room and looks around. Painted woodwork, chintz furniture, worn plank floors, rag rugs. A collection of odds and ends: a plastic white box fan, a metal TV tray, some kind of driftwood sculpture, a lamp whose glass base is filled with shells. Stacks of magazines are everywhere. Books line built-in shelves as well as the mantel and the small entertainment center that holds the modest television and stereo. There are a few sore-thumb heirlooms here, too—a gilt-framed oil landscape, an ornate coatrack, a stately grandfather clock. The windows are open, but the place still smells musty—kind of like the old books Calla buys at the library's annual sale back in Tampa.

It's as impossible to imagine her sophisticated mother in this setting as it is to imagine a sleek calla lily growing in that jumbled garden alongside the porch.

She can't help but think wistfully of their sun-splashed Florida home, with its contemporary furniture, central air, cool tile floors . . .

No. Don't think of the floor.

She closes her eyes to block out the vision of bright red blood pooling on the light-colored tile in the foyer.

A freak accident, the police said. Mom slipped or tripped at the top of the stairs, smashed her head open on the hard wrought-iron railing, and was probably knocked unconscious, meaning she never realized what was happening. What happened was that she broke her neck when she landed on the ceramic-tile floor in the foyer below.

The idea of Mom slipping—or tripping—is so bizarre that Calla still has trouble accepting what happened. Mom was the most coordinated, graceful, sedate person on earth. How could it have happened?

"So, obviously, this is the living room," Odelia is saying. "Through here is the kitchen."

Calla forces her eyes open and follows her huffing and puffing grandmother through an archway. Dark-green-and-white linoleum, white metal cabinets with silver handle pulls. What's visible of the countertop is pale green; most of it is obscured by canisters, appliances, a row of cookbooks and one of cereal boxes, a mug tree, a couple of empty vases, pens, paper, more magazines. The outdated fridge and stove are green as well, but they're more of an olive color. And yet another shade of green twines its way across the ivy-patterned wallpaper.

"Half bath here"—Odelia jerks open a door just long enough for Calla to spot a powder-blue toilet and matching sink in a tiny room with blue-and-silver foil wallpaper—"and this is my room." Odelia leads Calla through an open door into a bright room whose walls are mostly glass windows on three sides.

There are no curtains or shades, and the walls, trim, and ceiling are painted beige. On the floor is nubby neutral wall-to-wall carpeting, and the room is surprisingly—for this house, anyway—devoid of clutter. The only furniture is a trio of wingback chairs that seem oddly placed, all facing each other in the center of the room. On the lone table, at arm's reach, are a box of tissues, a couple of candles, and a tape recorder.

"This is your room?" Calla asks. "But where do you sleep?"

"Oh, it isn't my *bedroom*. That's upstairs. Come on—I'll show you yours, too. You're going to be in your mom's old room."

Mom's old room?

Calla immediately forgets about the one they're in and dogs her grandmother's footsteps back through the kitchen to the stairs. Predictably, the treads are worn and they creak as Calla and her grandmother ascend. Odelia is panting with exertion by the time they reach the second floor, where the ceiling is so low that Calla would be able to touch it from her tiptoes. The bare floor planks are wider, darker, scarred with age. The layout is simple: there are three doors off the upstairs hall. One, straight ahead, leads to a bathroom—Calla can see the edge of a clawfoot tub through the open door. But she isn't interested in that.

Nor is she all that interested in Odelia's room, to the right. She barely glances at the patchwork quilt–covered double bed; another overflowing bookshelf; and formal, antique-looking furniture that could only have been inherited, as it clearly isn't Odelia's style.

Finally, it's time to cross the hall to the opposite door, which, unlike the other two, is closed.

"This is where you'll be." Odelia reaches for the knob. "If you want privacy, close the door and I promise I won't come barging in on you."

"Er—thanks."

"But if you don't mind company, leave it open, and I'll know I can pop in. I was thinking it'll be nice to have someone to talk to around here for a change."

Calla nods, eager to see the room. Odelia is taking her sweet time opening the door, and it's all she can do not to bounce up on her toes to peer over her shoulder as it cracks open.

"I have to warn you, I haven't changed a thing since your mother left. Mostly because—in case you haven't noticed—I'm a sentimental, lazy old pack rat."

Then so are Dad and I, because we don't want to change anything of hers back home, either, Calla thinks. They made an unspoken decision before they left to keep everything of Stephanie's intact, right down to the last newspaper left on the kitchen table, folded open to the half-penciled-in daily word puzzle she loved to do. Neither of them could bear to put—much less throw—away anything Mom had touched.

"When I found out you were really coming to visit, I came in here thinking it was time I cleaned it out—but I just can't." Her grandmother's voice wavers, and Calla looks up to see tears in Odelia's eyes.

Unnerved, she looks down at her sandals. If Odelia loses it, she will, too. And she doesn't want her emotions to start spilling over again, isn't ready to go back to cheeks that are raw and stinging from perpetual salt and moisture, eyes that feel as though they've been boiled, the constant headache that accompanies incessant crying.

To her relief, Odelia inhales deeply, exhales, and manages a little laugh. Calla dares to look at her and sees that she's smiling as she gestures for Calla to step into her mother's room.

"At least Stephanie wasn't as messy as I am . . . how she ever got to be so organized and tidy, I'll never know. Anyway, I do dust in here, so you won't be sleeping with the dust bunnies, in case you were worried about that."

"I wasn't worried about that," Calla murmurs, and looks around.

The room is bright—not as bright as the back room downstairs, but sunlight splashes through windows on two walls. It falls in moving, dappled patterns across the hardwood floor and braided rug in shades of rose and sage. From here, Calla can see the glistening blue water of Cassadaga Lake.

She turns back to the room, wanting to take in every detail, trying hard to picture her mother here. It isn't easy. Mom's style is much more contemporary than this.

The walls are whitewashed beadboard halfway up and

striped wallpaper the rest of the way, in shades that match the rug. The furniture is strikingly similar to the bedroom set Calla picked out a few years ago when she redid her room back home, and she has a sudden memory of her mother commenting about that.

She had said something like, *"I had the same kind of bed when I was a little girl."*

To which Calla, feeling prickly, had retorted, *"Please, Mom, I'm not a little girl."*

No, but she feels like one now, and has ever since that horrible day when she found herself motherless.

A lump pushes its way into her throat, and she fiercely swallows it back down, focusing her attention on the details of the room. The bed is white iron, a twin, not a queen like Calla has at home. The dresser and nightstand are both painted white and rubbed off in a few places—the same distressed effect of her furniture back in Florida. But this stuff is authentically worn. Calla's set was purchased new—cottage-shabby-chic, the saleswoman called it.

"It's very popular right now," she told Calla and her mother, who, come to think of it, was wearing a faraway, nostalgic smile. Was she thinking of her girlhood bedroom? Missing this house in Lily Dale, missing her mother? Calla will never know now.

"I stitched this quilt myself." Odelia runs her fingertips over the patchwork squares that cover the bed. "I made it out of all her little-girl dresses."

Calla's eyes widen, and she steps closer to examine the various fabric patterns. Green-sprigged yellow rosebuds on a pale pink background, a red gingham plaid, powder blue and white pinstripes, an off-white eyelet.

"These were all my mother's clothes?"

Odelia nods, looking dangerously misty again behind her pink cat's-eye glasses. She turns to the window and jerks it open, muttering something about it being stuffy in here.

Calla smiles, imagining wrapping herself up in that quilt tonight. Maybe it will feel almost like a hug from her mother.

No. Of course it won't. Nothing—certainly not a quilt, and not even a real hug from her father, or her grandmother—could ever come close to bringing the kind of comfort she'd find in her mother's embrace.

She turns away from the bed, momentarily blinded by tears. She brushes them away quickly, and she can see again. Her gaze falls on a couple of framed photographs on the dresser. She steps closer and sees dated snapshots of her mother—younger, smiling—with various people she's never seen before.

Later, she'll ask Odelia who they all are, and hear the stories behind the pictures. Maybe she'll even ask her grandmother about that awful fight she had with Mom, and the reason they were estranged all these years.

Something about the lake.

But what?

Right now, Calla is simply too overwhelmed to even think about it.

There are a couple of magazines on the nightstand. Calla checks the date on the top one—*Mademoiselle*—and finds that it's more than twenty years old.

Not surprising. Odelia said she hasn't touched anything in this room. And judging by the stacks downstairs, Calla wouldn't be surprised if there are decades-old magazines there, too.

"I'll set the clock for you." Odelia gestures at the reddish orange digital numbers on the bedside clock, which are flashing 12:00. "Do you have a watch on?"

Calla shakes her head. She forgot the little bag containing her jewelry, including her cherished Movado watch, a gift from Kevin, back at home, along with a few other things she could have used. Like books from her summer reading list and tampons and her favorite coral-colored nail polish. It's not like she saw a super drug mart right around the corner, either.

"We lose power a lot out here at this time of year, whenever we get a bad bout of wind and rain," Odelia is saying. "I used to keep that clock set, but I stopped bothering years ago."

Calla looks past the clock to a little wooden chest. Its carved top is intricately scrolled in a floral pattern. Calla wonders if the bell-shaped blooms are lilies of the valley, her mother's so-called favorite flower.

"That's her jewelry box," Odelia informs her, and Calla is struck by a painful memory of the emerald bracelet—the one she lost in her mother's grave.

"It's nice." It would be nicer if it were etched with calla lilies. "Where did she get it?"

"I have no idea. She probably bought it somewhere when she was in high school—or maybe younger. I don't remember, exactly. There's nothing valuable in it, I'm sure . . . just trinkets and costume jewelry, that sort of thing. But whatever there is, you can have."

"Really? You don't want it yourself?"

Odelia smiles wryly and shakes her head, her gold chandelier earrings jangling with the movement. "Not my style."

"Well, thank you . . ." Calla trails off, uncomfortably aware that she can't bring herself to call her grandmother "Grandma."

Or even just "Odelia." Certainly not "Nana," which is what she called her other grandmother.

No, she doesn't know how to address this woman with whom she'll be spending the next few weeks, so she keeps settling on nothing at all.

"You're welcome."

Calla lifts the lid and is surprised when tinkling music spills out. She hears the sharp intake of Odelia's breath and her muttered, "That's odd."

"What is?"

"That the music is playing. I never wind that thing. I haven't done it since . . . in years," she finishes softly. Sadly.

For a moment, they listen to the delicate notes as the melody winds down.

"What is it?" Calla asks. "That song, I mean?"

"I have no idea. Why?"

"It just sounds kind of familiar. But I don't know where I heard it before." She looks down at the neatly organized contents of the jewelry box. Each satin-lined compartment is filled with earrings, bracelets, necklaces.

Mom always did love jewelry. But the real thing. The contents of her jewelry box back home in Tampa have been placed in a safe-deposit box while they're away. Someday, her father said, it will belong to Calla. Just like this.

But all she really wants is the lost emerald bracelet her mother gave her before she died.

The music has faded to silence; she starts to close the lid of the music box. As she does, she catches sight of her reflection in the mirrored panel in its top.

Somebody is standing just behind her.

She gasps and spins around, only to see that no one is there, and Odelia is already halfway out the door into the hall.

"I hope you're hungry," Odelia calls, "because I'm making my specialty for dinner. Spaghetti and meatballs."

Calla doesn't reply, just stares at the empty spot where she could have sworn somebody—not her grandmother—was just standing.

She didn't just see the human face, its features like those of an out-of-focus photograph; she also felt it. An unmistakable presence.

And now she feels a chill in the air that has nothing to do with the window Odelia just cracked open.

Is Odelia's house haunted? Or is it Odelia herself who's haunted—if there is such a thing?

Calla remembers the woman she saw at her mother's funeral—the woman in white, who was there one minute, gone the next. Her grandmother was with her when that happened, too. And what about the unexplained, overpowering flower smell outside?

Terrific. Odelia might not just be a harmless, eccentric old freak. She might be harboring ghosts, as well—spirits who hover around her like flies on a pig.

But people can't be haunted. Can they?

Who knows? Calla is pretty sure that she saw someone just now in the mirror. If Odelia isn't haunted, her house might be. Inside and out. But . . . what about the lady at the funeral?

Simple. The cemetery is probably haunted as well. It makes more sense for ghosts to hang around their graves than anywhere else. Not that Calla is sure that what she saw was a ghost, either time. One thing is certain, though: it wasn't her mother's spirit. That, she'd recognize beyond a shadow of a doubt. The woman in the cemetery in Florida was a stranger, and the face she barely glimpsed just now didn't seem familiar, either.

"Do you want to help me in the kitchen, or rest a little while before we eat?" Odelia calls as she begins to creak her way down the stairs.

"I'll help you." Calla hurries uneasily after her grandmother.

That's strange. It seems to be a good twenty degrees warmer in the hallway.

Feeling as though she's being watched as she heads toward the stairs, Calla can't help but wonder what she might see if she dared to throw a backward glance over her shoulder.

FOUR

After they've eaten dinner and washed and dried the dishes—
by hand, no dishwasher here—Odelia announces that she's
going upstairs to take a bath.

"I smell like a meatball," she complains, or rather just
observes, because that sort of thing doesn't really seem to
bother her.

Calla smells like a meatball, too, which *does* bother her. But
with only one tub in the house, she'll have to wait for her
grandmother to finish until she can get in there.

"Do you want me to wash the pots?" she asks, eyeing the
big skillet and kettle Odelia has soaking in one half of the
double sink.

"Nah, let everything soak until tomorrow."

Calla is struck, once again, by the stark difference between
her mother and her grandmother. Mom would have never,
ever left a pan in the sink overnight.

In fact, Mom would have never, ever let food get stuck in one of her pans in the first place—she was as conscientious about cooking as she was about everything else she did.

There's only one occasion that Calla can ever recall her slipping up in that regard. It was recently, too—back in March. Saint Patrick's Day. Calla is certain of the date because Mom had a soda bread in the oven. She made one every year, in honor of Dad's Irish roots—but only once a year, because she didn't like to bake with unhealthy white flour and sugar. Dad and Calla always looked forward to that soda bread, eaten with butter and jam.

This year, though, one of Mom's coworkers stopped by to give her a packet of information or something, just after she put the bread into the oven. Todd, or Tom—that was his name. Something like that. Calla remembers seeing him at the funeral.

That day, she answered the door when the bell rang, went to get Mom, and then the two of them disappeared into Mom's home office.

Calla remembers the smoke alarm going off a while later, when she was up in her room doing her homework. She ran downstairs to find that the visitor had just left and her mother was frantically opening all the windows in the kitchen, trying to fan out the smoke.

She was really upset—uncharacteristically so, Calla thought at the time. Mom was usually unflappable. That day, though, she was on the verge of tears as she dumped the burned soda bread, pan and all, into the garbage can.

Probably because she prided herself on paying the same careful attention to cooking that she did to everything else.

And because she had no patience for anyone who slacked off—least of all herself.

Unlike Mom, Odelia is—well, not so conscientious. About much of anything, as far as Calla can tell. But she's wildly creative. She put raisins in the meatballs and a pinch of brown sugar into the bubbling tomato sauce.

"I like things sweet," she informed Calla, who also likes things sweet . . . but spaghetti and meatballs?

It was surprisingly good, though. As she dug in, Calla found herself thinking she would have to tell her mother about the crazy recipe, before remembering that (a) her mother only makes a meatless sauce using fresh organic tomatoes, and (b) her mother is gone. Not to mention (c) her mother probably wouldn't be as amused as Calla is by Odelia's eccentricities.

Calla is really trying not to find her grandmother utterly charming, out of vague loyalty to her mother. Stephanie, after all, harbored some terrible, long-term grudge against Odelia.

But Calla can't help but get a kick out of some of the things her grandmother does. Not just putting raisins in the meatballs and brown sugar in the sauce, but also throwing a couple of strawberries into the glass of white wine she drank with dinner. Or counting to sixty, nine times—with a *Mississippi* between each painstaking number—while the pasta boiled to al dente, because her stove clock had broken and she never remembered to buy a new timer.

Now, Odelia is tucking a couple of cookbooks under her arm before heading upstairs to the bathroom. Seeing Calla's curious glance, she explains, "I do my best reading on the toilet."

"You read cookbooks on the toilet?"

"Sure," Odelia replies with a *Doesn't Everyone?* shrug. "Listen, help yourself to dessert if you don't want to wait until I get back downstairs. There are pecan sandies in the cupboard by the stove, and there's mango sorbet in the freezer."

Calla, who isn't quite sure what a pecan sandy is but happens to like mango sorbet, says, "I'll wait for you."

"Okay, but I might be a while. I like to soak in a nice, long, hot tub."

Yes, and read cookbooks on the toilet beforehand.

"You can entertain yourself, right?" Odelia asks.

Remembering at last to pose the question that's been nagging her throughout dinner, Calla replies, "Definitely, and I was wondering . . . where's your computer?"

"My *computer*?" Odelia snickers. "I keep it with my Porsche."

"What?"

"Honey, I don't have a computer."

"You don't?" Uh-oh.

I should have known, Calla thinks. But then, how could she have? Her grandmother is a virtual stranger, and Calla had no way of knowing that Lily Dale would be so . . . old-fashioned.

If only she'd been able to talk her parents into buying her a laptop for her birthday in April, instead of just an iPod. Not that she doesn't like her iPod, but a lot of good it will do her now, when it comes to staying in touch with her friends back home.

This is just crazy. How is she supposed to live through a full three weeks without e-mail and the Internet?

"I thought you had your own computer," Odelia says. "I remember you being on it in your room an awful lot when I was down there."

"I do have one, but it's a desktop." Seeing Odelia's blank look, and wondering how anyone in this century can be so clueless, she clarifies, "It's not portable—not a laptop."

"Oh. That's a shame."

A shame? It's a crisis, as far as Calla is concerned.

Really? A crisis?

Ashamed of her reaction to what really amounts to an inconvenience in the wake of a true crisis in her life, she forces herself to say, "It's okay, I'll just learn to live without being online for a while."

"I guess you don't have any choice. Sorry, honey."

"It's okay. At least I've got my cell phone."

Odelia hesitates, as though she wants to say something about that. Then, thinking better of it, she shrugs and goes upstairs, humming what sounds suspiciously like OutKast's "Hey Ya!"

Calla listens. It *is* OutKast's "Hey Ya!" Not exactly the most current song, but at least it's from this century. Now, if Odelia could just update herself on technology as well . . .

Shaking her head, Calla takes her cell phone from her pocket. Calling Lisa will make her feel better. Wait until she hears about—

Huh? She raises the phone closer to her eyes and frowns. *No service?*

Maybe it's because she's in the house. She takes the phone out onto the front porch and checks again. Still nothing. Not in the street, either, or halfway down the block.

She returns glumly to the house. Now what?

There's always her iPod . . . but if she listens to music, she'll find herself thinking. And if she allows herself to do too much thinking these days, her thoughts take her to dark places. She'll wind up crying again. She doesn't want to start crying, because she might not stop.

She'll have to keep her thoughts occupied, then. For now, she'll find something to read and take it out to the porch. She brought along a couple of books from home, but she's too lazy to go upstairs and get them.

Too lazy? Come on.

All right, she's . . .

Well, not exactly scared. Just a little . . .

Spooked.

Did she see a ghost earlier, upstairs? Did she see one in the cemetery that day? Will she see one again now?

Does she even believe in ghosts?

No. Of course not.

She is, after all, the daughter of a very practical banker who wasn't big on abstract thinking. Mom didn't go to church or discuss ethereal topics like religion; she didn't even encourage Calla to believe in Santa Claus, much less God. She didn't actively discourage it, but when Calla asked if Santa was real, Mom would say things like, "Consider the evidence. Have you ever seen him? Not the department-store guys in the fake beards, but the real thing, sneaking down the chimney in the middle of the night."

"We don't have a chimney."

"Exactly."

"And isn't it too hot here for reindeer and a sleigh?"

"What do you think?"

Calla wanted to believe in Santa Claus, but she couldn't find the evidence, so she reluctantly let go. She was six. God, she still believed in—secretly. Because she really needed to.

Mom, who liked to equate seeing with believing, obviously didn't. It isn't hard to imagine what she'd say about ghosts.

Alone in the living room, Calla quickly turns on the seashell lamp. Artificial light helps to banish the late-day shadows cast by the dying sun that just barely reaches the windows.

Seeing a mirror on the opposite wall, Calla walks decidedly toward it.

Will I see a ghost in my reflection again?

No. It's just me.

There she is, looking like her usual self, if a little thinner than usual. Her arms look bony, sticking out beneath the sleeves of her white T-shirt. And her jeans are riding too low though her belt is buckled in the last hole; she needs either to find a smaller belt or to start eating more.

Tonight, she realizes, was the first time she's had much of an appetite lately. She even had two helpings of spaghetti. Odelia had four and didn't even bother to do the whole "I really shouldn't, but I can't resist" routine typical of most women, like Lisa's mom, Mrs. Wilson.

Odelia was as unapologetic about overeating as she was about her choice of bathroom reading material—or the fact that she reads on the toilet in the first place.

Calla sees herself smile in the mirror as she contemplates her grandmother's many quirks.

Then her smile fades and she looks long and hard at her reflection and beyond, wondering if she'll spot anything—or anyone—unusual in the room behind her.

Nope. Nothing at all. And the air temperature seems to be holding steady as well.

Okay. So maybe what happened upstairs was her imagination.

Or maybe the temperature really did drop and she really did see a ghost.

But even if that's the case, the ghost isn't here now. Calla's alone in the room—of that, she's certain.

Turning away from the mirror, relieved, Calla begins browsing the nearest row of books. Most of them appear to be romance novels, with a couple of new-agey nonfiction titles thrown in. She's reaching for one of those when she hears something through the screened window at the front of the house.

Footsteps crunch up the path, up the wooden steps, across the porch. The bell rings.

Now what?

Calla walks to the foot of the stairs. She can hear water running up there.

Should she answer the door herself or ignore it?

As she turns toward it, she sees that she has no choice. A figure is standing right there, watching her through the window in the old-fashioned door.

Not a ghostly figure, or one that's the least bit ominous, thank goodness. It's a roly-poly middle-aged woman. Probably one of her grandmother's friends.

Opening the wooden door but leaving the screen door securely latched, Calla smiles expectantly. "Hi."

"Er . . . hello." The woman's expression is a little strained. Her face is drawn, and there's a telltale red puffiness around her eyes. Calla recognizes it, having seen the same thing in her own reflection often enough these past few weeks. This woman has been crying.

"Is Odelia Lauder in?" she asks in a way that makes it clear she's not a friend of Calla's grandmother's. Nor does she know much about her, Calla assumes, when she goes on to ask, "You—you're not her, are you?"

"You mean am I Odelia? No! I'm her granddaughter." Calla notices then that the woman isn't alone. Someone is hovering in the shadows beside the porch steps, standing right in Odelia's flower bed, actually. That strikes Calla as odd, and rude. It might not be the most manicured garden, but that doesn't mean people are welcome to stomp on the blossoms.

"My name is Elaine Riggs," the woman says, not bothering to introduce her companion, who appears to be a teenage girl, judging by her slight build, slouchy clothing, and long hair. "Is Odelia here? I was wondering if she could do a reading. My friend Joan sent me. She said she's really good."

Calla blinks. "Excuse me?"

Now the woman—is she the girl's mother?—looks equally confused. She takes a few steps back toward the edge of the porch, leans back, and glances up, toward the eaves, as if checking something. The girl she brought with her doesn't move. Calla can feel her stare, though she can't make out her features in the twilight.

The woman gives a little nod, saying, "This is Odelia Lauder's place . . . she isn't in, then?"

"No, she's in . . . she's just, um . . . busy." Calla wishes the woman would tell her daughter to get out of the flower bed. Talk about rude.

But she continues to ignore the girl as she asks, "So she isn't doing readings tonight?"

Doing readings? What on earth is this woman talking about?

"I just drove five hours from Columbus. I probably should have called first, but . . . I guess it was a whim. Joan said Odelia takes walk-ins . . . and . . ." The woman falters.

Walk-ins? Is her grandmother a hairdresser or . . . a doctor? *If she were, I'd know it*, Calla thinks. On the heels of that, she realizes she has no idea what it is, exactly, that her grandmother does for a living. She must support herself somehow. Odds are, though, that she isn't a hairdresser or a doctor.

The woman is still waiting, the girl still staring silently from the flower bed. Calla shrugs, for lack of anything constructive to say. She isn't about to admit that she has no idea what her grandmother's job is. Nor is she about to invite these strangers inside. Something about the girl is giving her the creeps.

"I . . . she's really busy right now. I don't know what to say."

"All right. I'll come back tomorrow. I can't drive all the way back alone tonight anyway." Dejected, the woman turns and heads down the steps.

The girl stays where she is as the woman walks right past her without acknowledging her. Then, after seeming to give a little nod at Calla, she turns and walks away, right through the flowers, not caring that she's probably trampling the whole bed.

Standing in the screened door, Calla watches them head down the street. The woman glances from house to house like she's looking for something or someone. The girl walks a few steps behind her. They aren't interacting. That's odd.

Maybe they had an argument or something. And the woman did say she'd be driving alone. Maybe the girl lives somewhere else.

Speaking of odd . . . what was the woman looking at above the porch? Curious, Calla unlatches the door and steps out into the twilight. She walks over to the edge of the porch, looks up to see what the woman might have been looking at, and finds herself staring at a wooden sign hanging from a bracket on the porch roof. She hadn't even noticed it earlier.

Now, peering up into the gathering dusk, she can't quite make out from this angle what the lettering says, other than her grandmother's name.

Hmm. Calla goes down the steps to get a better view and looks again at the sign. There. Now she can see the whole thing:

ODELIA LAUDER, REGISTERED MEDIUM

It's all Calla can do to drag herself back into her grandmother's house after reading that crazy sign out front.

Registered medium? Classic whack job is more like it.

Mom was right about her mother. Odelia is off her rocker—and now Calla's stuck here with a kook who puts raisins in meatballs and advertises herself as some kind of fortune-teller. Or whatever.

Back in the lamplit living room, Calla paces past the bookshelves and back again, their contents forgotten. She longs to keep on walking, right out the door, but she can't do that.

Where would she go? She's stuck in the middle of

nowhere. It's not like she can hail a cab or take a bus or even call someone to come pick her up. Lisa is a thousand miles away. And now her father's on the opposite side of the country.

In fact, he should be calling any minute now. He promised he would when he lands safely in California. He's going to want to know how everything is here.

What will she tell him?

That Odelia is a con-artist freak and lives in a haunted house?

What, exactly, does a so-called medium do, anyway? Or *claim* to do?

Calla's never come across one before, and Mom would never let her watch any of those supernatural television shows or movies about ghosts and hauntings. She said they were ludicrous. And once, when Calla stupidly told her there was going to be a Ouija-board seance at Tiffany Foxwood's slumber party, Mom made her stay home. Lisa's mother did the same, which wasn't surprising because she's so religious. Calla was surprised Mom wouldn't budge, though.

"If Ouija boards are so stupid and fake, why do you even care?" she asked her mother.

"Because I don't want you to get caught up in ridiculous things like that. You have better things to do with your time and your brain."

"Last week you let me go to Amber Cunningham's nail-painting party. That's just as ridiculous and you had no problem with it."

"Fine. Then the next time you're invited to a nail-painting party, you're not going."

Talk about an unsatisfactory answer. Sometimes, Calla couldn't figure out her mother.

But I'd give anything for another chance at it, she thinks glumly, then drags her thoughts back to the present before the grief can kick in again.

Calla's pretty sure a medium supposedly has supernatural powers; some kind of paranormal connection to the spirit world. And if Calla had ever stopped to think about what kind of person might make such a claim, Odelia would probably have popped into her head.

Look at her, with those flowing clothes, that wild red hair, and all that jangling jewelry. She looks like some kind of gypsy. Is it so surprising that she'd act the part as well?

Okay, you are so not being fair, Calla tells herself guiltily. *You can't decide a person is a freak—or a con artist—just because of how they look.*

All right, then . . . to give Odelia the benefit of the doubt, Calla wonders if she might actually be able to talk to the dead. Is that really so far-fetched?

After all, weren't you just thinking you had seen a ghost right here in this house?

A chill slips down Calla's spine, even as she reminds herself that her mother wouldn't buy into this ridiculousness—any of it—for a second. Mom had too much common sense. If she were here right now, she'd be telling Calla to use her head and weigh the evidence.

Since there isn't any evidence that can't be explained away as a figment of one's imagination . . .

That's probably all any of this is. Then again . . .

Wait a minute.

Calla stops pacing, struck by the coincidence. Can there possibly be a connection between the ghost Calla saw—*no, the ghost you* thought *you saw*—upstairs and her grandmother's claim to be a medium?

Oh, God. What if she really is a medium?

In the grand scheme of things, isn't it pretty unlikely that Calla, who has never seen—or *thought* she's seen—a ghost in her life, would suddenly bump into one here, now, today?

It's not as if she can blame it on the power of suggestion. Until a few minutes ago, she had no idea her grandmother even claimed to be a medium.

Whoa. She paces more quickly, fists clenching and unclenching at her sides.

Okay, so then . . . maybe Odelia *is* a medium. And maybe this place is crawling with ghosts.

Yeah. Good going. Nothing like completely creeping yourself out.

What if there are dead people hanging around her grandmother's house, waiting for their chance to try to make contact with her?

Why would I be able to see them, though? I'm not a medium. Unless . . .

A thought barges into Calla's consciousness and refuses to budge. A thought so preposterous that it steals away her breath:

What if that sort of thing—talking to ghosts—runs in families? Like height or eye color? What if Odelia really is a medium . . . and so am I?

FIVE

"There you are!"

Calla hastily wipes the tears from her eyes, then looks up to see her grandmother, wearing a pink towel turban and a fuzzy orange robe, peeking through the bedroom door. She left it slightly ajar—not because she welcomes Odelia's company, but because she still can't shake the memory of the figure she glimpsed here earlier.

"I was waiting for you downstairs—I found the front door open, so I figured you must have gone out for a walk."

Oh, that's right. She forgot to close it after that startling discovery about Odelia, and came up here to fight off that troubling suspicion about herself.

But it's stubbornly managed to stick for the past half hour or so as she lay on her mother's bed and stared at the ceiling.

"So . . . did you go out?" Odelia asks.

"No."

"You just opened the door?"

"Right."

Odelia pauses, then asks, "Mind if I ask why?"

"You mean, why did I open the door?"

Odelia nods.

"Because some lady rang the doorbell." Calla forces herself to look her grandmother in the eye. "She said she wanted you to do a reading."

"What did you tell her?"

She can't read her grandmother's expression.

"I told her that you were busy."

Odelia nods. "That's fine. I was."

Calla returns her gaze to the ceiling. She can feel her grandmother's eyes on her.

After a moment, Odelia says, "You're wondering what a psychic reading is, aren't you."

It isn't a question.

And the straightforward, dead-on comment catches Calla off guard.

"Yes," she admits. "I mean, I think I know. But I don't know why the woman thought *you* could do one for her . . . unless . . ."

"I'm a psychic, Calla."

"I thought you were a medium. That's what your sign says."

"All mediums are psychic, although not all psychics are mediums."

Calla shrugs, not sure what her grandmother expects her to do with this information.

"So you saw my sign, then. Is that how you figured it out?"

She nods.

"I didn't think you knew before you got here, and I wasn't sure how to bring it up. Your mother never mentioned it to you, did she."

Again, not really a question.

"No, she never mentioned it."

But she did happen to mention that you were a classic whack job.

"Well," Odelia says with a wistful tilt of her red head, "I'm sure it wasn't something she was very proud of."

Calla is sure she's right about that. Her mother was a straight arrow, which is probably why she and Odelia wound up at odds.

Then again . . . *the lake.*

Something about the lake . . . that was why they'd had that last big argument.

She glances out the window, where the water is visible through the trees. Earlier, it was a sparkling, inviting blue.

Now, shrouded in twilight, it's an ominous shade of purplish black.

What was it about the lake?

"What did your mother tell you about Lily Dale?" Odelia intrudes on her speculation.

"Just that it was a small town. And cold. And it snowed a lot."

Odelia smiles. "That's true. Winter settles in by late October and it doesn't let go of us until April or May."

"May!"

"It snowed on Memorial Day weekend a few years ago."

Calla finds herself shivering at the mere thought of that. She's seen snow only once, when her parents took her skiing in Utah.

Rather, *they* skied. Calla stayed in the chalet with an elderly babysitter who didn't mind playing Candyland over and over again—though Calla minded. She remembers asking why they couldn't go outside and build a snowman or make snow angels. The sitter said it was just too cold, and Calla's disappointment was as pervasive and bitter as the January mountain wind.

"Do you think it'll snow while I'm here?" she asks her grandmother.

"I doubt it. Then again, you never know."

"You're supposed to be a psychic, aren't you? You must know everything. Don't tell me you can't predict the weather." It comes out laced with sarcasm. Calla can't help it. This is all just way too much to grasp.

"Oh, psychics don't pretend to know everything."

"No? What is it that they do pretend?"

Ignoring that, Odelia continues, "Every human being has psychic potential, you know. Some people are just born ultra-sensitive to earthly energy vibrations around them, and they choose to—or sometimes, inadvertently—learn how to interpret them."

"So, what's a medium, then?"

"A medium is tuned in to other kinds of energy as well—not just earthly. Spirit energy is paced differently—faster, higher—if that makes any sense at all."

It doesn't. But Calla is fascinated anyway, hanging on her grandmother's every word—and doing her best not to show it, out of some loyalty to Mom, who would hate this conversation.

"Think of it like a sensitive radio that's capable of tuning in to a frequency other radios might not be capable of receiving. A medium is basically just a highly responsive transmitter, receiving signals others can't pick up and passing them on."

"Yeah, but radios don't pick up signals from dead people."

"Around here, we prefer to say Spirit."

Around here? We? Her grandmother must have a bunch of imaginary friends—or so-called spirits—living in her house. Or, more likely, in her head.

Nonplussed, Calla mutters, "Dead is dead."

"There is no such thing as 'dead,' Calla. People who have departed their physical bodies on this earth are still with us. They never really leave us. If you can believe that, you'll find a great deal of comfort."

Calla bows her head and blinks away hot tears, thinking of her mother.

She wants to lash out at her grandmother: *Mom's not still with me, because if she were, I'd feel her.*

I can't feel anything at all. She's just . . . gone.

Odelia comes over to the bed, sits on the edge of the mattress, and touches Calla's shoulder. "Listen . . . I know this isn't easy for you. Any of it. But I do think you'll find some comfort in Lily Dale, and maybe even get to like it here, if you give it a chance."

"I'm already giving it a chance, aren't I? I'm here."

"Right. You're here. But you didn't know about us before you came."

"Us?" Calla echoes blankly. "What do you mean, *us?*"

Odelia hesitates. "The thing is . . . I'm not the only medium in town, Calla."

"You're not?" she asks slowly.

"No. There are lots of us. Dozens, in fact, now, during the season, so—"

"Dozens?" Calla interrupts, stunned. "How can there be dozens of mediums in a tiny town like this? What kind of crazy coincidence is that?"

"It isn't a coincidence at all. Lily Dale was founded back in the eighteen hundreds as a center for spiritualism."

Thud. Calla feels as though she's been flattened by an eighteen-wheeler.

Finally, she recovers enough to ask, "So, the whole town is . . . haunted?"

Odelia laughs. "I guess you could say that . . . but *I* wouldn't."

"What would you say?"

"That the town is filled with caring, sensitive folks using God-given gifts to help people."

"Help them how?"

"There are any number of ways. Healing, counseling, communicating with Spirit. Some of us have different areas of expertise."

"You mean, like doctors have different specialties?"

Odelia looks pleased. "Right. Like that."

"So, what's your specialty?" Calla asks, deciding to at least act as though she's buying into this stuff. Maybe there's a part of her that does—or, at least, is willing to try.

"Oh, I'm a jack of all trades, you could say."

"But you can see dead people? Spirits?" she amends. "Talk to them? And get messages?"

Odelia nods. "That's exactly it. And it's taken me many years of training to figure out how to interpret those messages from what they show me. Even now, there are times when I don't get things exactly right."

"So, you don't actually hear them speaking?"

"Sometimes I do."

"What do they sound like?"

"Well, sometimes I just hear my own voice in my head, in their words. But I usually do hear my guides' voices. And they sound much higher-pitched than a human voice . . . they're on another wavelength, basically, to put it into layman's terms."

"What are guides?"

"Spirit guides. They're entities that are a permanent part of us all, but they exist on a higher realm. Everyone has them, but not everyone can see them."

"You mean, they're like guardian angels?"

Odelia looks pleased by Calla's question. "In a way, yes."

"What about my mom? Is she my spirit guide now?"

Odelia hesitates. "She might be. Some who cross over continue to guide their loved ones from the other side. But spirit guides—the kind I'm referring to—aren't on the earthly plane."

"How do we know they're there, then?"

"Oh, they're there. You can learn to become aware of them through meditation—they'll become known when you're receptive to them. Or sometimes, if you need their help but aren't even aware that you do—or that they exist—they'll try to get your attention somehow."

"How? By popping up and saying 'boo'?"

Odelia ignores her sardonic tone. "They have different means of letting you know they're there. They can show up physically or let you hear them, or smell—"

Impatient, Calla cuts in. "What about my mom? Can she do that, too?"

"Calla—"

"Can you see her and talk to her?"

"I haven't."

"Why not?"

Odelia shrugs, looking reluctant to answer. "Some people come to me after they pass, others don't. Mediums can't always see people closely connected to our personal lives. And when I do readings, I tell people there's no telling who is going to come through to them. It might not be who they're hoping to get, but it's always who they're meant to hear from."

"What's that supposed to mean?" Calla, increasingly irritated, doesn't wait for a reply. "Are you saying that if you did a reading for me, you might put me through to, like, the old guy from down the street who died when I was a baby, and not to my mom?"

"That's exactly what I'm saying."

"That's stupid."

"Calla—"

"I mean, if you can't put someone through to the person they want to talk to, then what good is any of it?"

"It's not like a telephone," Odelia says evenly. "It doesn't work like that. You can't just place a call to the other side and ask to speak to someone specific."

"Then why even bother getting a reading at all?"

"You probably shouldn't."

"That's fine, because I wasn't planning on it. I don't even believe in it, anyway," she feels compelled to add, for good measure. Even though it might not be true.

She waits for Odelia to defend her so-called profession. She merely shrugs. "That's your prerogative. Your mother didn't believe, either, for what it's worth. And neither did her father."

Odelia's talking about Calla's grandfather, Jack Lauder. Mom never talked about him. All Calla knows is that Mom's parents split up when she was a little girl, and her father moved away and had little to do with Odelia or Mom after that.

Maybe now I know why, Calla can't help thinking. *Because his ex-wife was a whack job who thought she could talk to dead people—only, just random dead people. Nobody who matters.*

"As for *your* father," Odelia goes on, "I'd be willing to bet he still hasn't got a clue what I do, or that this town is populated by registered mediums."

"I'll bet you're right. Because if he knew . . ."

"You wouldn't be here," Odelia finishes for her when she trails off. "Right?"

"Right." Her father would have her on the next plane out of here, even if it meant giving up his sabbatical in California. No way would he let her stay in a crazy place like this. It was hard enough to persuade him to send her here in the first place.

"Are you going to tell him?" Odelia asks her after a moment. "When he calls?"

"Are *you?*"

"Not unless he asks."

Calla finds herself smiling despite herself at the thought of her father happening to inquire, *"Say, by any chance is this Lily Dale place filled with people who can talk to ghosts?"*

"So . . . are *you* going to tell him?" Odelia asks again.

74

Calla hesitates. "No. Not unless he asks."

Odelia smiles at her. She isn't in the mood to return it, though.

"Want some milk and cookies? I always have that before bed. And mango sorbet."

Calla shrugs and swings her legs over the edge of the mattress. "Why not."

"Oh, hi, Jeff. Sure, she's fine . . . no, everything went fine . . . yes . . . yes . . . hang on a second, she's right here." Odelia turns to Calla, sitting at the table spooning the last bit of melting sorbet from her plastic bowl, and holds out the telephone receiver. "It's your dad."

Calla knew that, of course. She knew it when the phone rang.

So, does that make me psychic? Ultrasensitive to earthly energy vibrations around me?

No. It's just common sense. He wouldn't have been able to reach her on her cell, so of course he'd try Odelia's number.

"Dad?"

"How's it going, hon? I tried to get you on your cell phone but I kept getting voice mail. I left a few messages, but I didn't want to wait to talk to you. I miss you too much already."

Calla is completely caught off guard by the tsunami of emotion that sweeps through her at the sound of his voice. For a second, she can't even speak.

She watches Odelia dunk another pecan sandy, which turned out to be a delicious shortbread-tasting cookie, into a glass of milk.

Then she manages to croak, "My cell doesn't get service here."

"Uh-oh. Will you survive?" He doesn't wait for an answer. "So, your grandmother did meet you at the airport on time . . . right?"

Calla knew before she left that he doesn't think Odelia is the most responsible human being in the world. Back in Tampa, he kept asking her if she had cash for a cab, just in case her grandmother was late—or didn't show up at all.

"Yup, she was there, right on time." Calla watches her grandmother finish the cookie in two bites. "How was your flight, Dad?"

"Late. Crowded. Bumpy." He sounds beat. "I hope yours was better."

"It was."

"Good."

Oh, ick. Odelia is pouring Hershey's syrup on another helping of sorbet. Chocolate and mango aren't the ideal pairing as far as Calla is concerned, but Odelia gobbled up the last serving, so maybe she's on to something.

"So, everything's okay there?" Dad is asking. "Other than the cell phone not working?"

She hesitates for the slightest fraction of a second. "Definitely."

"What's the town like?"

"Small. Cute." *Haunted.*

"How about the house?"

"The same." *In every way.* She shivers a little.

Seeing her, Odelia murmurs, "It's getting cold in here, isn't it? I'll shut the window."

"So, you think you're going to be okay there," her father asks, "until September?"

September.

Wow, when he puts it that way, Calla isn't so sure she's going to be okay at all. Homesick, she merely nods before he says, "Honey?" and she remembers he can't see her.

"Yeah, Dad, I'm going to be fine here. I just wish . . . I mean, I can't get online here, either. There's no computer. So, that's a little . . . disappointing."

She sees Odelia lift her head abruptly. She assumes it's because of the computer comment, but she realizes Odelia doesn't even seem to be paying attention to her conversation. Her head is cocked expectantly, almost as though she's listening to something. Or *for* something.

"Maybe there's an Internet café there or something," her father suggests as she watches Odelia set down her spoon, wearing a thoughtful expression.

"Here? Um, no." Where does her father think she is, in civilization?

"Well, what about the library? Sometimes they have computers the public can use. You need to check it out."

Suddenly, Calla sees a shadow pass through the open doorway behind Odelia's head, where the door to the sunroom is propped open by a doorstop.

There's someone in there. Only . . .

There shouldn't be anyone there at all. Calla and her grandmother have been sitting here for twenty minutes, eating sorbet and talking. Odelia never once mentioned anybody else being in the house. And surely she would have.

If she knew about it.

Even as Calla looks on, her grandmother turns her head sharply toward the sunroom.

"Calla?" her father is saying in her ear. "Why don't you check out the library?"

"Right. I will."

"Good. Let me know what you find out. I'll talk to you tomorrow."

"Tomorrow?" she echoes absently, her attention on her grandmother, who has stood and walked to the doorway of the sunroom.

"I'll call you around this time tomorrow night, okay?"

"Mmm-hmm," Calla murmurs.

Odelia is talking, so softly Calla can't hear what she's saying. She suspects that's because her grandmother doesn't want her to hear.

"I love you, Calla."

"I love you, too, Dad."

She hangs up the phone.

"Who are you talking to?" she asks her grandmother.

Odelia doesn't turn around right away. When she does, Calla expects her to deny that she said anything, but she shrugs. "That's just Miriam."

"Miriam? So there is someone there?"

Odelia's eyebrows shoot up. "You saw her?"

Something makes Calla shake her head promptly and say, "No. I didn't see anybody. I just heard you talking, so I thought someone was there. So," she adds tentatively, her heart pounding like crazy, "who's Miriam?"

"She's just someone who used to live here, years ago."

"Before you moved in?"

"Long before that." Odelia gives a staccato laugh. She crosses to the window above the sink, gives it a tug, and pulls it closed. "She lived here long before I was born, actually. Her husband built the house in eighteen eighty-three."

Calla feels as though a giant just stepped on her lungs, squashing the air right out of them.

"So . . . Miriam's a ghost?"

"She's passed, yes," Odelia tells her. "I don't use that word."

"Ghost?"

"Right."

"Sorry." Calla takes a deep breath and asks, "Is she your spirit guide?"

"No. Not a guide." Calla watches her grandmother turn back to the other room, then say, "All right. I will."

She's talking to the ghost, Calla realizes, and the pale hair on her arms stands straight up.

Odelia returns to the table. "Miriam wanted me to tell you that she's harmless."

"Oh. That's . . . good to hear."

"She just likes to keep an eye on things around here."

"Is she . . . always around?"

"Not twenty-four seven. She comes and goes. You won't notice her. Most people don't, although . . ."

When Odelia breaks off, Calla prods, "Although what? What happened?"

"She gave the plumber a scare last fall. She kept turning the lights on and off and flushing the toilet to get rid of him."

"Why?"

"She just didn't like him."

"Why not?"

"Who knows?" Odelia shrugs. "I'm sure she had a good reason. When she tells me something, I've learned to listen. So I waited until my regular plumber got back to town and used him, and everything was fine."

Calla nods as though all of this makes perfect sense, because she's starting to feel exhausted, mentally and physically, and it's just easier than posing endless questions.

But she does have one more. "Is Miriam the only ghost around your house, then?" Oh, wait—Odelia doesn't like that word. "I mean, is Miriam the only person who's, uh, passed, and is still hanging around here? Or are there other, uh, passed people, too?"

"Spirit energy is all around us."

"All the time? And, uh, you mean, around all of us? Not just . . . people like you?"

"All the time, all of us . . . everywhere."

Whoa.

"Those of us who are sensitive to it learn how to tune in and out, though. If we didn't, we'd go nuts."

I should be sitting here thinking you are *nuts,* Calla tells her grandmother silently, *only for some reason, you're almost making sense.*

"Want some more sorbet?" Odelia offers the carton to her. "There's a little more left. Finish it up."

"Oh . . . no thanks."

"Try it with chocolate sauce. It's better that way."

Calla makes a face. Now that's nuts. "That's okay." She pushes back her chair. "I think I'll go to bed."

"That's a good idea. It's been a long day."

And it's going to be a long three weeks, Calla thinks as she makes her way through the strange little house and up to her mother's old room.

SIX

". . . The only way we'll learn the truth is to dredge the lake!"

With a gasp, Calla bolts upright in bed, clutching the covers against her pounding ribcage.

The room is dark. And filled with unfamiliar shapes—Oh. She's not home. She's in her grandmother's house, in her mother's old room. Mom is gone.

And Calla was dreaming about her. About her grandmother, too.

They were arguing shrilly. Calla was a little girl, eavesdropping, pretending to play with her dolls under the table.

The only way we'll learn the truth is to dredge the lake!

What did that mean? Which of them said it, Mom or Odelia? Did it really happen, or did Calla make it up in her dream? And why does it matter?

I don't know, but it just does. There must be a reason it keeps coming back to me.

Breathing hard, she lowers herself to the pillow again and tries to relax.

Snippets of the dream conversation come back to her.

"*. . . because I promised I'd never tell. . . .*" That was Mom, distraught, tearful.

"*. . . for your own good. . . .*" That was Odelia.

"*. . . how you can live with yourself. . . .*" Odelia again.

None of it makes any sense. Not in fragments, anyway. If Calla can slip back into the dream, she might be able to piece it all together.

But that doesn't work. Sleep eludes her; she's wide awake now. It's cold in here, but that's not because of any ghost. It's early August, yet she can feel the chill coming through the open window with the night breeze.

She glances around the room just in case, though, making sure none of the shadows look human. She's relieved to see nothing but the bulky geometrical outlines of furniture.

At least the resident ghost—Miriam, Odelia called her—doesn't seem to be lurking here at this hour of the night. Or morning. What time is it, anyway?

Calla glances at the clock. The glowing numerals, no longer flashing, show that it's 3:17.

Her grandmother must have come in to set the time. It was still stuck on 12:00 when Calla came up to bed, and she hadn't bothered to fix it, too preoccupied with all that had happened.

She did, however, shut the door behind her.

If you want privacy, close the door and I'll leave you alone.

Yeah, right. Calla can't help but feel annoyed that Odelia went back on her word so quickly. She doesn't like the thought of anyone opening the closed door and creeping in here while she was asleep, even if it was just to set the clock.

Then again, maybe she should be glad it was only Odelia. When she first came up to bed earlier, she was so uneasy about the face in the mirror—among other things—that she expected to toss and turn all night. She must have fallen right to sleep, though, because the last thing she remembers is turning off the light and sinking into the pillow.

Now, all those anxious thoughts come at her full force once again, each more difficult to believe than the last.

There's a ghost in the house? Lily Dale is filled with mediums? Odelia is one of them?

Finally . . .

What about me? Why can I see and hear and sense the same things she does—like Miriam? Do I have supernatural powers, too? Am I psychic?

That thought wants to make a whole lot of sense to her—if only she would accept it. But she does her best not to.

That's crazy. I can't be psychic. I'm a regular person.

Then again . . .

All right, the thing is, Calla has always had a way of anticipating things she shouldn't—*couldn't*—know about in advance. Usually, it's just everyday surprises that catch other people off guard. Like a pop quiz in biology or an underdog team winning a game. Sometimes, though, she wakes up just knowing something isn't quite right. Something in her own life. Something major.

That happened to her back in April, just before Kevin sent her that breakup text message out of the blue. It struck again in May—not another electronic breakup, but the inexplicable sensation that something bad was going to happen. She was powerless to figure out what it might be, let alone stop it. She just knew it was out there, lurking, waiting to happen to her.

And then Mom died.

What if she had told Mom about the bad feeling she had that morning? Would that have changed anything?

She still remembers feeling uneasy as she ate her cereal, watching her mother gulp down a cup of coffee and pack up her briefcase for an early meeting. But she didn't realize the bad feeling had anything to do with Mom. It was mostly just a vague sense of dread, which she didn't mention because Mom didn't want to know about those kinds of things. She had made that clear years ago.

One morning, back in elementary school, Calla faked a stomachache. She doesn't remember clearly why she did it, only that she knew she shouldn't go to school. Mom had to scramble her schedule to stay home with her, and she wasn't happy about it.

That afternoon, they found out there had been a fire at her school. Everyone was evacuated safely, but it was pretty scary for the kids.

Shaken, Calla confessed to her mother that she wasn't really sick, that she had pretended because she had a feeling something bad was going to happen at school that day.

She remembers that long-ago conversation clearly because her mother's reaction was so disturbing—and so strange. It wasn't that she was angry Calla had lied about being sick, and it wasn't that she was the least bit skeptical, either. It was more that she was upset that Calla had had a premonition in the first place.

"Just keep it to yourself," Mom said sternly. "Promise me that you won't tell anyone about this. Or anything like this, if it ever happens again. You have to promise!"

"But why?"

"It might make people upset. Even Daddy, so don't talk about it to him either, okay?"

"But what *is* it? What happened to me?"

"It's just . . . women's intuition," Mom replied, and laughed a little hollowly when Calla protested, "But I'm not a woman!"

She's still not a woman, age-wise, anyway. But somehow, she does seem to have women's intuition, frequently able to feel vibes other people, like Lisa, don't even realize are there.

Is she now picking up on things other people can't see or hear or smell, too? *Ghosts?*

Good Lord. She can imagine what her mother would say about what's been going on since she got here.

Wait a minute. Mom lived for years right here in Lily Dale, with Odelia, in this very house. She had to know Odelia is a medium and that the town is devoted to the supernatural.

Okay, so why didn't she ever tell Calla and her father about it?

Maybe she did tell Daddy, Calla considers—before quickly dismissing that idea. If Mom had mentioned any of this to him, Calla wouldn't be here now. Period.

Maybe I should have told him right away, when he called, she thinks guiltily. *Maybe I should tell him now.*

She looks again at the clock. 3:19. What time is it in California? Past midnight, she realizes with regret. Too late to call.

I will in the morning, though, she decides, turning over and closing her eyes resolutely.

He might make her leave.

Might?

He'll definitely make her leave.

So what?

Anything would be better than staying here with a kooky grandmother in a haunted house . . . right?

Burrowing into the quilt made from her mother's little-girl dresses, Calla feels the soft fabric against her cheek and experiences a pang of regret.

If she leaves, she won't get to sleep here in her mother's old bed, in her old room. She won't get to know her mother's hometown, or Odelia.

If she leaves, another connection to her mother—and the past—will be severed.

Is that really what you want? Calla asks herself. *I don't know. I don't know what I want.*

She only knows what she *doesn't* want: to see another ghost. Unless, of course, it's her mother. Then again . . .

I don't want Mom to be a ghost. I want her to be real. I want things to be back to the way they were.

When at last Calla drifts off to sleep again, it's on a tear-soaked pillow.

In the morning, she calls Lisa long-distance from her grandmother's kitchen phone. Without permission. But only because her grandmother isn't available to ask, she tells herself. She also tells herself that Odelia won't mind. And that she'll pay her back for the charges.

"Calla! I've sent you, like, fourteen e-mails and left a zillion voice mails. Where have you been?" Somehow, Lisa's drawl seems more pronounced than Calla ever noticed in person.

"I've been here. I just can't get online yet and my phone doesn't have service."

"Why are you whispering? Is your grandmother still sleeping?"

"No, she's up," she says in a low voice, glancing at the closed door to the sunroom.

She heard the doorbell ring a little while ago, as she was coming out of the upstairs bathroom. She stood still in the hall, trying to eavesdrop on her grandmother's conversation with whoever was on the porch. Then the screen door squeaked open and banged closed, and voices and footsteps faded to the back of the house. When Calla came downstairs a few minutes ago, the sunroom door was closed.

She's positive Odelia is in there, giving a reading. It's an educated guess—not a supernatural premonition or whatever you call it when you just know things.

What she can't begin to even guess is what time it is. The clock in her room was flashing 12:00 again when she woke up, the stove clock in here is broken, and she can't tell much by looking outside at the angle of the sun because there is no sun today. It's a depressingly gray day. Warm, muggy air seeps in through the windows Odelia has opened throughout the house.

"What time is it?" Calla asks Lisa. *And why isn't my clock still set? Was there a storm in the night? Did the power go out?*

"It's almost eleven thirty," Lisa informs her. "Why?"

"Eleven thirty! I can't believe I slept so late."

"Wow. You just got up? You must be really relaxed up there."

"Not exactly. It's . . . more the opposite." She quickly

explains to Lisa, in a hushed tone, with one eye on the closed door, what's been going on. She doesn't go into the creepy "dredging the lake" comment—which, after all, might not even be a recollection but a mere dream. She also instinctively neglects to tell her friend about the ghost she herself glimpsed.

She's glad she didn't mention that part when she hears Lisa's response to the news that Odelia—and, reportedly, everyone else in town—sees and talks to dead people.

"What a bunch of freaks! You need to get out of there, before you get into trouble."

"Like what?"

"Who knows? With all those freaks running around, there's no telling what can happen."

"Well, where am I supposed to go? My dad's in California now."

"You could come back here. Please, Calla. I miss you so much."

"I miss you, too. But I can't come back. There's no place for me to—"

"You know my mom said you're always welcome."

Yes, she knows. She also knows Kevin is still home from college. Then again . . .

She can't help but remember how right it felt when he touched her arm that day in the cemetery. Or how he told her to let him know if she needed anything.

She does. She needs familiarity. She needs Kevin and Lisa and . . . home.

"What abou—" She breaks off, takes a deep breath, and allows herself to ask Lisa, "What about Kevin?"

There's a pause. Never a good sign.

"What *about* Kevin?" Lisa asks. "He's here. That's about it."

It isn't like her to speak so tersely about her adored older brother. There was a time, when they were much younger, when Lisa's nonstop "Kevin this" and "Kevin that" drove Calla crazy. Then Calla fell for him, and she and Lisa had even more in common.

After the breakup, Calla alternated between warning Lisa that she didn't want to hear a thing about Kevin to pumping her for information. Lisa was willing to oblige in either case.

Now that the wound isn't so raw, Calla finds herself curious about him and asks Lisa cautiously, "What has he been up to lately?"

"Mostly bugging my parents to buy him a car to take to school. And I think they might actually do it, too."

"That would be good."

"Yeah, only then he'd have to drive all the way back up north alone, and my parents don't want him to do that." Lisa changes the subject. "So listen, if you came back down here, you could sleep in our guest room and finish school at Shoreline like you were supposed to. We'd get to be like sisters, living in the same house and everything. Remember when we were kids and we used to pretend that we were?"

"Sisters?" Calla smiles. "Yeah, only nobody ever believed us."

"I was hoping one day we'd be sisters-in-law, you know?" Lisa says unexpectedly, and quietly. "Then my brother had to go screw that up."

"Lisa, don't—"

"I'm sorry. I can't help it. I just miss the way things were."

Yeah. She's not the only one.

"And I miss you, Calla. I wish you'd come back and stay here."

"How can I if Kevin's around?" Calla stares at the overcast sky through the window above the kitchen sink. "Wouldn't that be awkward?"

"I guess it would," Lisa says reluctantly, "especially since— oh, never mind."

"Since what?"

"I hate to tell you this, but I feel like you should know. . . ."

"Know what?"

"Kevin's new girlfriend. He, uh . . . has one. And she's coming down to visit."

Ah, the sucker punch. How can Calla be caught off guard, though? She *knew* he was seeing someone else. Again, an educated guess. Or maybe a psychic vision. Women's intuition or just plain old-fashioned logic.

When you're suddenly dumped after two years, chances are you've been replaced.

"Look, maybe," Lisa is saying, "you and I could go away somewhere while she's here. We could, you know, visit Tiffany. She's at her family's house on Sea Island till school starts." That means September. Shoreside Day starts late, for Florida—not until after Labor Day.

"No!" Calla's tone is curt. She can't help it. "No way am I going to visit Tiffany. And no way am I going to live under the same roof as Kevin. I just . . . I can't."

"I'm really sorry, Calla," Lisa says softly. "I promise to hate her when I meet her."

Good old loyal Lisa.

"So . . . who is she?" Calla hears herself ask, though she isn't sure she really wants to know. "Does she go to Cornell with him?"

"I guess so. She's from Vermont or New Hampshire or something. Her name is Annie."

Annie. Only adorable, sweet, nice girls are named Annie. Everyone knows that. Well, Calla knows it, anyway.

So let Kevin live happily ever after with adorable, sweet, nice Annie. That's fine with her.

She'll just go on doing exactly what she's doing, right here in Lily Dale.

If only I knew what it is that I'm doing here in Lily Dale. Yeah, that would help.

"Hey, Calla? Do you want me to hop on a plane and come see you this weekend? I feel like you need me. And that way, I wouldn't have to be around to meet Annie."

"I doubt your parents would let you come."

"I'd make them let me if you needed me."

Calla smiles. Lisa is pretty good at getting her way. She has her parents wrapped around her pinky—that's what Kevin always used to say, anyway.

Kevin. Her smile promptly evaporates.

"Listen, Calla, I'm serious. Let me know. Because I'll get on the next plane if you need—"

"Thanks, I'll let you know," Calla cuts in hurriedly as the door to the back room begins to open. "Lis', I have to go."

"Okay, but remember—"

"I'll call you soon, okay? 'Bye."

She hangs up just before Odelia emerges with the woman who was here last night. The one from Columbus, Ohio. Only this time, she's alone. She looks like she's been crying again.

"Well, good morning, starshine." Odelia reaches out to give Calla's arm a little pat as she passes her at the table. She again has on that pair of too-snug lemon-yellow capris and a lime-green shirt emblazoned with a glittery silver turtle. It all clashes with her red-orange hair, which also clashes with her hot pink lipstick and turquoise earrings. "I'm just going to show Mrs. Riggs out, and I'll be right back."

Calla nods, then does a double take. She could have sworn only her grandmother and Mrs. Riggs were there, but now she sees that there's someone else. A girl—the same one who was standing in the flower bed last night.

Only now, Calla can see her more clearly—though it's only a glimpse in passing before the three of them disappear into the hall. She's about Calla's age, pretty, with long blond hair and baggy clothing. She doesn't glance in Calla's direction, and she trails silently behind Odelia and Mrs. Riggs as they leave the room.

Calla shivers, then remembers that just a few minutes ago, she was thinking it was warm and muggy in here. She hears the front door open and close. Moments later, Odelia is back in the kitchen. "I didn't peg you for a late sleeper, but I'm glad you are."

"I had no idea what time it was when I got up. The clock is blinking again."

"Oh . . . I still have to set it for you, don't I?"

"I can do it this time. But thanks for doing it last night."

"Last night?" Odelia frowns. "I didn't set it for you last night."

"You didn't? But . . ."

But she woke up in the middle of the night, and the clock was set. She distinctly remembers that it said 3:17.

"I thought you must have come in and set it sometime in the middle of the night," she says slowly, even as she realizes uneasily that it is warm and muggy in here after all. Or . . . again.

"Oh, I don't do much of anything in the night. I sleep like a rock. Anyway, like I said, I don't believe in opening closed doors on other people. I wouldn't do that even if I thought you were sleeping."

"Thanks," she murmurs. "I just . . . wondered. About the clock. It isn't set now, and—"

"Listen, you're not on a schedule here, so relax. You're on summer break—that's what it's for. Stay up late. Sleep in. I don't get up till noon myself most days, if I can help it."

"Noon?" Calla echoes, wondering if it's possible that she imagined it all. Was the whole thing a dream, not just the clock, but the remembered—or manufactured—conversation about dredging the lake?

"Noon," Odelia confirms. "And I like to take a nice long afternoon nap in my recliner if I don't have anything scheduled." She pours herself a cup of coffee and looks expectantly at Calla. "Want some joe?"

"Oh . . . uh, no thanks." That would be the day Mom or Dad would ever offer her coffee. "So . . . you do readings every day? Walk-ins?"

"Sure. During the season, anyway. I'm pretty booked."

"People just show up at the door, like just now? What do they want, specifically?"

Odelia mimes pulling a zipper across her sealed lips and shakes her head.

"You can't talk about your clients?"

"I try not to. What happens in Vegas"—she tilts her head toward the sun-splashed back room—"stays in Vegas."

"So that's . . . what? Your office?" Calla asks her, pointing at "Vegas."

"More or less. It's where I see people when they come to me."

It's hardly a candlelit Victorian parlor, which would seem more fitting. As far as Calla can recall, there's no crystal ball in there, no round table with a fringed cloth, no heavy draperies, not even incense.

"Sometimes," Odelia continues, "I go to my clients, though. And sometimes I do my thing out at the stump, or the auditorium."

"Did you say 'the stump'?"

Odelia grins. "Inspiration Stump. It's out in Leolyn Woods."

"A tree stump?"

"It used to be. Now it's encased in a concrete block. You'll learn more about it if you stay."

"*If* I stay?" Calla echoes.

Her grandmother walks over to the cupboard and takes out a loaf of Wonder bread, saying, "I know you're having second thoughts, sweetie pie."

How do you know? Calla wants to ask, but thinks better of it. Of course she knows. She's psychic.

"And I'm not surprised you're thinking of getting the heck out of Dodge," Odelia goes on. "You were hit with a real wallop yesterday when you found out about me, and Lily Dale."

Calla nods. A wallop. Yeah, you could call it that.

And what about the fact that her mother and grandmother never got along? Why didn't they? Did it have anything to do with Lily Dale, and Odelia's so-called occupation?

The lake. It was something about the lake . . . dredging the lake? Already, last night's dream—no, nightmare—is beginning to fade.

"Look, I'm not going to try to persuade you to stick around"—Odelia opens the fridge and removes a carton of eggs—"but I'd like it if you would. It's been nice, having you here with me. I get lonely sometimes."

"Doesn't Miriam keep you company?" Again with the sarcasm. But Calla can't seem to help herself, and anyway, Odelia doesn't bat an eye.

"Miriam can't eat my cooking, and she can't play Trivial Pursuit. How about you?"

"What? I, uh, liked your spaghetti and meatballs," Calla admits with a weak smile.

"I hope you'll like my French toast, too, because that's what I'm about to make us for breakfast. Are you good at Trivial Pursuit?"

"That depends—which edition?" Not that it matters much. Sometimes, when she plays—rather, *played*—with Lisa and Kevin, she found that the answers would just come to her, even when she had no clue about the subject matter.

"Genus edition, of course," Odelia says briskly. "Want to play after breakfast?"

Calla shrugs, unaccustomed to playing board games in the middle of a weekday—or eating breakfast at nearly noon. "Sure," she says, "why not. But what about your schedule?"

"Unless I get another walk-in, I'm free for a couple of hours."

"So you can't even tell me why they were here?" she asks, curious about Mrs. Riggs and her daughter.

"Why who was here?"

"That woman, Elaine, and her daughter. From Ohio."

Odelia is staring at her, looking surprised for some reason. *Oh! She must think—*

"They were the ones who were here last night," Calla quickly explains. "That's how I know they're from Ohio. The mom told me. She told me her name, too."

Just so you know I'm not some kind of . . . psychic.

Odelia is wearing an oddly thoughtful expression, watching Calla carefully. "Did her daughter tell you her name, too?"

"No. She didn't say anything."

Odelia nods. Still staring. Feeling uncomfortable, Calla changes the subject. "Um, I had to make a phone call to my friend in Tampa. I hope that's okay. I'll pay for the charges."

"Hmm?"

"The long-distance charges. I would have asked, but you were busy with those people."

"Right." Odelia nods slowly. "The woman and her daughter. From Ohio."

"Right."

"Oh, don't worry about the charges." Odelia has finally snapped out of it. Whatever it was. "It was probably just a few cents. No big deal."

"Are you sure?"

"Positive."

Calla gets the feeling her grandmother wants to say something more, but she doesn't.

SEVEN

A few rainy days later, in yet another lunchtime Trivial Pursuit tournament—now a tradition—Calla has four wedges of proverbial pie in her game piece. Odelia has five and is madly rolling the dice in an effort to gain the sixth.

"Roll again . . . four! History or roll again. I'll roll again." There's a knock at the door as she blows on the dice.

"Who is it?" she calls, shaking the dice in both hands, her gaze intent on the game board.

"It's me, Odelia," a voice calls through the screen door.

"Oh, Evangeline!" Odelia stops shaking, hands poised over the board. "I forgot all about you. Come on in!"

"Thanks a lot," the voice retorts, and the screen door creaks open. "You tell me to come over as soon as I get back from camp, and then you forget about me?"

A moment later, a young girl with frizzy reddish hair appears in the living room.

Another client? Nah, Calla decides, taking in her rather plain, pudgy face and realizing they must be around the same age. Evangeline's wearing a pair of baggy khaki shorts and an oversized orange Cleveland Browns T-shirt, and her sturdy, athletic-looking legs end in purple high-top sneakers worn without socks. Calla can't tell if she's truly heavy or just looks that way because of her clothes. Lisa the fashionista would love to do a makeover on someone like her.

"This is Evangeline Taggart, Calla. She's our next-door neighbor."

Though she's still not sure about being in Lily Dale, Calla finds herself pleased when her grandmother says "our," as though she's genuinely part of the household.

"Evangeline's been away at camp for a week," Odelia says. "How was it?"

"Boring. As usual. But my brother liked it, so that was good. How do you like Lily Dale so far?" Evangeline asks Calla.

"It's nice." Not that she's seen much of it. The weather has been lousy and her grandmother has had back-to-back appointments every morning, afternoon, and evening. She's been encouraging Calla to venture out and explore on her own, but she hasn't felt like it.

All right . . . maybe she's still a little spooked.

Mostly, she's been moping around, brooding about her mother and the school year that lies ahead, reading her way through Odelia's stacks of novels or writing letters to Lisa. Real letters, not e-mail. Not that she has much to write about. Funny how it's a lot easier to write an e-mail about nothing than a real letter about nothing. E-mail is less permanent, so what you're saying doesn't seem to matter as much. It's all about the connection.

Never in her life has Calla felt so . . . *disconnected*.

"Game over." Odelia sets the dice aside and checks her watch.

"Don't quit on my account," Evangeline says. "I don't mind hanging out, watching."

"I know, but that's okay. We're done. I've got a client coming in ten minutes."

"Don't you want to at least finish your turn?" Calla asks her grandmother.

"No, thanks. I was going to roll a three. That wouldn't have helped me."

"She's hard to beat at Trivial Pursuit," Evangeline comments, peering over the board. "But, wow, look at you! Four pieces of pie. You gave her a run for her money, didn't you?"

"I know a lot of trivia," Calla explains lamely.

She doesn't miss the questioning glance Evangeline shoots at her grandmother, nor Odelia's shrug in response.

Calla finds herself jealous of their bond, and disturbed by the unspoken communication between them. Evangeline was clearly wondering whether Calla, too, is psychic.

Odelia obviously isn't sure. But why not? What would make her think Calla *might* be?

She doesn't know about the apparition Calla saw in her mother's room that first night, or about the premonitions she's had in the past.

Maybe I should tell her, Calla thinks, not for the first time. *Or maybe I should just forget about all of it, or I'll start acting as crazy as Odelia.*

She opts for the latter. At least for now.

"Evangeline, how about if you show Calla around this afternoon?" Odelia suggests briskly. "The rain is letting up, finally."

"Sure. Do you want to look around, Calla?"

There's nothing to do but smile at Evangeline and say politely, "Sure."

Well, it's either that or announce that she has no interest in sightseeing in this spooky little town, which isn't exactly the case, anyway. She's curious about Lily Dale, she'll admit that. Because her mom grew up here, and because . . . well, she can't help but be intrigued by the idea of a town filled with psychic mediums.

For some reason, though, she hasn't wanted to ask her grandmother much about it. Maybe because she's afraid of what she'll say. Or ask in return.

"So, what do you think about Lily Dale?" Evangeline asks as she and Calla stroll away from Odelia's beneath a gloomy sky.

"I haven't even seen it. We've been inside the house since I got here the other day."

"Well, this is Melrose Park." They're crossing a grassy, tree-shaded green, heading away from the murky waters of the lake. There are people strolling here and there. Most of them seem to be women of all ages, usually in pairs or groups. Some are clutching pamphlets and stopping to consult them, as if they're looking for something.

"I'll show you where the Assembly office is first," Evangeline decides.

"What's the Assembly?"

"The Lily Dale Assembly. For spiritualism. Hang on a second, I've got to tie my shoe." Evangeline stops and stoops over her purple sneaker.

Calla seizes the opportunity to look around at the quaint, close-set nineteenth-century gingerbread cottages. They're architecturally similar to Odelia's, some well kept, others run-down. Most have equally chaotic flower beds, and never in her life has she seen so many outdoor ornaments. Wind chimes, birdbaths and birdhouses, flags and banners, garden gnomes . . .

She's about to comment about that to Evangeline when something else catches her eye.

Signs. They're old-fashioned shingles, really, just like the one that hangs from Odelia's porch. And they're nearly as abundant as the wind chimes, which, in a sudden gust off the lake, are tinkling to life.

PATSY METCALF, REGISTERED MEDIUM
& SPIRITUAL CONSULTANT

REV. DORIS HENDERSON, CLAIRVOYANT

ANDY BRIGHTON, PSYCHIC MEDIUM

One house even has a pair of shingles, hanging one above the other:

WALTER DARWIN, REGISTERED MEDIUM

PETER CLIFFORD, HEALER

Wow. The whole place really is crawling with . . . freaks.

Evangeline, standing again, follows Calla's gaze. "That's where Jacy lives." She gestures at the neat little house with double signs.

"Jacy?" Calla realizes he's the guy she met just after she arrived.

"Yeah, he's this guy . . . he's pretty new here, too. He came from Jamestown, but before that he lived on a reservation down on the southern tier."

"Reservation? You mean like—"

"He's Native American," Evangeline explains.

Oh. Not Cuban after all, Calla thinks. *Native American.* She knew he had to have exotic blood, with those unusual good looks.

Evangeline goes on, "I'm sure you'll meet him soon."

Calla opens her mouth to tell Evangeline that she already did, but Evangeline is the chatty type and rarely pauses for a breath. "I saw him heading toward Leolyn Woods before, when I was coming across the yard to your grandmother's. Walt and Peter are his foster dads. You have to meet Jacy. He's really cute."

Now that it seems to be her turn to speak, Calla tries to think of something else to say. Something other than, *I'm not interested in meeting cute guys.*

Her thoughts shift automatically to Kevin. Kevin and his new girlfriend. Annie.

All right, so maybe Calla should be interested in meeting cute guys after all.

Then—as if called up by her consciousness—one happens to materialize right in her path at that very moment. Not Jacy. Another cute guy. Maybe the cutest guy she's ever seen.

Evangeline stops short. "Oh, Blue! You scared me!"

"Sorry." He's not looking at Evangeline, though. His eyes—the same deep indigo shade the lake was yesterday, in the sunshine—are fastened on Calla.

"I'm Blue Slayton," he says, and sticks out his hand.

She takes it and finds his grasp strong and sure, though his hand is a little cold and dry for a warm, sticky day like this.

"Hi. Nice to meet you." Calla tries not to stammer, unnerved by her own sweaty palm and his good looks. His light brown hair is wavy, and she has the strange urge to run her fingers through it. She releases his hand and shoves hers into her pocket, not just to wipe off the moisture, but in case it's tempted to stray his way again.

"She's Calla, Odelia's granddaughter from Florida," Evangeline tells Blue, and Calla realizes she forgot to introduce herself. "It's Delaney, right?" she adds, and Calla nods.

"Hey, I'm really sorry about your mother." Blue Slayton's words catch her off guard.

"So am I," Evangeline chimes in awkwardly, "but I wasn't sure if I should bring it up."

"It's okay," Calla murmurs, wondering just how many people in Lily Dale are aware of her circumstances. Probably just about everyone, she realizes, if Odelia has been talking about her. After all, it's a small town. People in small towns like to gossip, don't they? She wouldn't know, never having lived in one. But judging by the way both Blue Slayton and Evangeline Taggart are looking at her, they both know a lot more about her life than she knows about theirs.

"Your grandmother's glad you're here," Evangeline offers. "At first, she didn't think you were really going to be able to come, because of your dad. But I guess it's good that he's going to California and you can't go with him right away. He had no choice where to send you, huh?"

Sheesh, Calla thinks. *Does she know my shoe size and grade point average, too?*

She says nothing to Evangeline, just does her best not to sneak another peek at Blue. She can feel him watching her with those amazing eyes. She wonders if his parents named him Blue, or if it's just a fitting nickname.

"So, how long are you sticking around town?" he asks, and she looks up.

Wow, he really is gorgeous. Even better-looking than Kevin. More sophisticated, too, despite Kevin's new grown-up haircut and attitude.

Why is he staring at her? He seems to be waiting for something.

Oh! He asked her a question. What was it?

She backtracks to *How long are you sticking around town?*

"Until, um . . ." How long *is* she sticking around? Distracted by his stare, she searches her sluggish brain for the information.

"You're here until the beginning of September, right?"

"Oh! Right," Calla says, grateful to Evangeline for bailing her out.

"That's good," Blue tells her, barely glancing Evangeline's way. "Maybe we can hook up at some point while you're here."

Hook up? Does hook up mean the same thing here in Lily Dale that it does back home?

She dares to sneak another glance at his face, sure someone

like him can't possibly be interested in her. But his expression sure makes it look that way.

Hmm. Maybe *hook up* means the same thing everywhere.

Her heart pounds a little faster as she says, "That would be good."

"Good. See you around, then." He gives a little wave and takes off.

"OhmyGodheissototallyintoyou!"

Calla shifts her focus from the departing Blue Slayton to Evangeline.

"Just so you know?" Evangeline goes on, bouncing a little on her purple sneakers, "Blue Slayton is the hottest guy in the Dale. Not that there are all that many guys here, but . . ."

But Blue Slayton would be hot anywhere, as far as Calla's concerned.

"Plus," Evangeline tells her, "he just broke up with his girlfriend, so he's available."

"Oh. Well, that's . . ." Calla trails off, not sure *what* it is. Encouraging? Scary?

Both, she decides, but says only, "too bad. About the breakup, I mean. Breakups are hard."

They start walking again, and Evangeline asks, "So, you don't have a boyfriend, do you?"

You mean Odelia didn't cover that breaking news? Calla thinks wryly, kicking a stone with the toe of her white Ked. Wait— would her grandmother even know about Kevin? Calla didn't mention it when Odelia was in Florida, and she doubts her father brought it up, either. They certainly had other things, far more traumatic things, on their minds then.

"No," she says in answer to Evangeline's question. "No boyfriend. Not anymore."

"Nasty breakup, huh? Like you said, they're hard. Especially when you get dumped for somebody else."

Calla looks up sharply. "How do you know?"

"Not from experience—I've never had a boyfriend myself—but that's what just happened to my aunt Ramona. Her boyfriend was cheating on her with some Buffalo Jills cheerleader with blond hair and huge—"

"No, I meant how do you know what happened to me?"

"I was right, huh? Sometimes I'm off, but I'm getting better."

"You mean you're . . ." *One of them?*

"Clairvoyant. Yup." Evangeline looks pleased with herself. "It runs in my family. Same thing with Blue. His dad's David Slayton, the guy who solved that jewelry theft after the Oscars in L.A. last year, with that actress . . . what was her name?"

Calla, stunned into silence, doesn't answer. She knows exactly what Evangeline is referring to. Anyone who watches TV or reads *People* magazine knows about that. A movie star had borrowed a million-dollar diamond necklace to wear to the Academy Awards. It disappeared even though the jeweler's security detail was on her all night. At first, there were rumors of a publicity stunt by the actress or the jeweler himself.

But the case was solved a few days later when the necklace was found. One of the security guards turned out to have been in on it. A psychic hired by the actress claimed to have helped the police solve the case. Calla remembers seeing him on TV and thinking he looked like a movie star himself.

Blue's father. Wow. She asks Evangeline, "So Blue is . . . ?"

"A medium. Right. Like his dad."

"And . . . so are you?"

"Yup. My whole family is. My brother, Mason—he's thirteen—and my aunt Ramona, who we live with. My parents were, too, until they died."

"Both of them? How?" Calla blurts, and is immediately sorry. She, more than anyone, should know enough not to force Evangeline to talk about something so painful.

But her new acquaintance merely nods and says, matter-of-factly, "It was a car crash out on Route 60, in a blizzard. Mason and I were with them, but he was a baby and I was only two, so I don't remember any of it, thank God."

"I'm so sorry." Horrible as it is to have lost her own mother, at least Calla had her for all these years—and still has her father.

She shudders at the thought of being orphaned, and suddenly misses her father. A lot.

What if something had happened to him, too, and she had to stay with Odelia forever?

"It was a really long time ago," Evangeline is saying. "But believe me, I sort of know what you've been through, with your mom and everything. I miss my mother all the time."

"So you can't just . . . connect with her?"

Evangeline raises an eyebrow. "You mean, as a medium?"

"Right."

"Sometimes I feel her, and I hear her in my head."

"You don't see her?"

"I haven't. My father, either. But I don't need to see my parents to know that they're with me. And actually, I don't have to be a medium to talk to them."

"But . . . they talk back, right?"

"Usually."

"My grandmother said it doesn't work that way. She said it's not like a telephone where you can just place a call to the other side and get in touch with someone."

"She's right. It's not. It's more complicated than that. Sometimes, it's the opposite of what you might think. Like, you know, you aren't always in touch with spirits who are close to you." She pauses. "It's just . . . hard to explain, to someone who doesn't have the gift."

"Yeah? Try me."

Evangeline's hazel eyes darken. "You seem skeptical."

"I am. I mean, my grandmother said the same thing—that she can't just get in contact with my mom whenever she feels like it. But she claims that she can communicate with all these other random spirits, like the lady who used to live in her house."

"Miriam. Right. She can. And I've seen her, too. She's been around for years. She pops in next door, too. She was the first apparition I ever saw."

She might be mine, too, Calla thinks—before she remembers the strange woman in the cemetery in Florida. She's pretty sure that wasn't Miriam, though her recollection of the woman's features isn't very clear. She sure would have taken a much harder look if she'd had any clue that she was seeing a ghost.

Maybe you weren't, a little voice—a skeptical little voice— pipes up in her head. *Maybe you're just imagining stuff now that you know about Odelia and Lily Dale.*

Then again, she saw the figure in the cemetery—and the one in the mirror here—before she knew there was anything supernatural about the house or town, let alone her family bloodline.

She realizes Evangeline is watching her thoughtfully.

"Listen, Calla, I know it's not easy to be plunked down in a place like this, and I don't blame you for doubting, really. I guess I'd feel the same way if I hadn't grown up here."

"You've never lived anywhere else?"

"Nope. My parents were mediums, like I said. And so were their parents."

"So it runs in your family."

Evangeline nods. "But not in yours, right? Is that what you're thinking?"

Calla shrugs. "Nobody in my family other than my grandmother goes around saying they're a medium, if that's what you mean."

"Well, you never know. Maybe they just don't want to admit it."

"They . . . who?"

"The other people in your family."

"There is no one else. Not on my mother's side, anyway. My grandmother had a sister, but she died a few years ago. I never knew her, but she didn't live here, anyway. She lived in Rochester. And I never knew my grandfather—they were divorced years ago. And then there's my mom, but she definitely wasn't . . . you know . . . a medium."

"Are you sure?"

"Positive," Calla says firmly, remembering how Mom told her to keep her "women's intuition" to herself. "And I'm not a medium, either." *Sheesh, Calla, why don't you just say "So there," and stick out your tongue?* But she can't help it. She can't

111

let herself buy into this whole supernatural scene just because she's here and it's apparently a way of life for these people.

Now it makes sense that Mom never brought her and Dad to Lily Dale. The weather is lousy most of the year, but the summer months are "the season." Mom wouldn't have wanted Calla and her father exposed to all that.

She was the most pragmatic person Calla's ever known. And it doesn't take a so-called gift to know what Mom would say if she were here right now. She would tell Calla to use her common sense. And common sense tells her there's no such thing as ghosts, and you can't communicate with the dead no matter how desperately you want to reach your lost loved one.

Even Odelia and Evangeline seem to back up that part of the theory.

"Come on." Evangeline glances at the sky, then picks up her pace. "We should get moving. We've got a lot of ground to cover before it rains again."

"Maybe it won't." Calla spots a few broken patches of blue amid the clouds.

"No, it will."

"Psychic vision?"

"No, meteorological tradition." Evangeline smiles demurely. "I've lived here all my life, remember? Western New York isn't exactly known for its balmy weather, Sunshine State Girl."

Again, Calla is overtaken by homesickness for Florida. But she's not even going home after the summer. No, instead, she'll be headed to another strange place. And by the time she gets back to Tampa, she'll be on the verge of going away to college. All her friends will be moving on, too. And Mom will still be gone. The old life she longs for no longer even exists.

"Are you okay?"

She looks up to see Evangeline watching her, concerned. "Yeah, I'm fine."

Sorry, Mom, she thinks silently. *Sometimes you can't help telling a lie.* She only wishes she honestly believed her mother could hear her.

"I didn't mean to bring it up."

"Bring what up?"

"Florida," Evangeline says simply. "I know it's hard. And if you ever need to talk . . . I'm a good listener."

"Thanks," Calla says, wondering if she's just made her first friend in Lily Dale.

EIGHT

Ninety minutes and a drenching downpour later, Calla is soaked through, and knowledgeable enough about Lily Dale to understand what Evangeline means when she says, "See you at message circle some night, right?"

"I'll try." Calla waves and starts up her grandmother's porch steps before remembering to add, "And thanks for everything. It was great getting a personal walking tour."

"Enjoy this place while you can. Once the season ends, it's desolate around here." Evangeline said earlier that the local population will shrink drastically after Labor Day. Most of the registered mediums board up their cottages and hang CLOSED UNTIL JUNE signs, spending the cold-weather months in warm-weather places. "Oh, wait, you won't be here then, anyway."

No, she won't. The *season*, Calla now knows, is July and August, when Lily Dale's gatehouse is occupied. Nonresidents have to pay to come into the town, where they can attend a daily schedule of events: seminars, workshops, services, lectures, group readings. People who want a private reading or healing session but haven't scheduled an advance appointment are free to wander up and down the streets, knocking on doors of spiritualists in residence here. The streets are filled with people who are grieving or sick or at some crossroads in their lives.

It's hard for Calla to believe that this is where they turn for comfort, but judging by the number of registered mediums in town, spiritual counseling is a booming business.

"Hey, don't forget," Evangeline calls after her, "you can come over to our house whenever you want to get online."

"Thanks, I will," she says gratefully.

Calla was dismayed to find out that there's no public Internet access here in Lily Dale. The Maplewood Hotel's lobby is wireless. She's out of luck without a laptop to use there. But Evangeline said Calla can check her e-mail on her aunt's computer anytime.

"It was really nice of you to show me around, Evangeline."

"No problem. It was fun." With a wave, Evangeline disappears into the house next door.

It was *fun,* Calla thinks as she walks up the path toward Odelia's porch, wondering if her grandmother ever locks the door. Maybe she doesn't bother because it doesn't do much good when you're dealing with the spirit world. A deadbolt wouldn't stop the likes of Miriam.

Terrific, now you're starting to think like they do, Calla scolds herself. Maybe that's because Lily Dale has turned out to be more ordinary—at least, on the surface—than she expected.

The locals who were out and about today could live in

Anytown, USA, as far as she can tell. She wasn't sure who was a medium and who wasn't unless Evangeline pointed it out, and even then, she was often surprised.

The ordinary-looking, balding middle-aged man on a ladder washing the windows of his cottage over on Cleveland Avenue was a world-renowned clairvoyant, which means he can see into the future. The word, Evangeline explained, literally translates from French into "clear seeing."

Meanwhile, the elderly woman decked out in a black felt hat and some sort of cloak, who looked for all the world like she must live in a haunted house, turned out to be nothing more than a local busybody who works for the post office and supposedly steams open other people's mail.

The cute, freckled, pigtailed little girl with holes in the knees of her jeans recently channeled a dead president. The dumpy housewife without a shred of supernatural talent is having an affair with a volunteer fireman who does past-life regression in his spare time.

Calla couldn't help but be fascinated by Evangeline's accounts of their private lives—paranormal, extramarital, and otherwise. In some ways Lily Dale could be any other small town in the world, if you ignore the shingles that dangle from many of its houses. Calla is almost used to them now. *Almost.*

ODELIA LAUDER, REGISTERED MEDIUM

That one still catches her off guard as she passes beneath it on her way up the steps.

She glances at the spot where that girl—Mrs. Riggs's daughter—was standing the other night, in the middle of

Odelia's flower bed. To her surprise, the dense growth of flowers there shows no sign of being disturbed. You'd think the stems would be snapped or crushed or something.

The front door isn't locked, as Calla suspected. When she lets herself in, her grandmother is nowhere to be found, and the door to the back room is closed. Hearing the rumble of voices, she figures Odelia must be in there with a client.

All right, then, she'll go upstairs and do some reading. She heads to her room, a few books from the Lily Dale library tucked under her arm. Evangeline helped her find some local nonfiction titles on the history of Lily Dale and spiritualism. She checked them out on Evangeline's card, not wanting to get one of her own just yet despite the librarian's invitation.

There's just something so . . . permanent about a library card.

Calla isn't opposed to spending a few weeks here in the Dale, as the locals call it. But it isn't her home, and she isn't trying to make it feel that way. She isn't prepared to make herself at home in a place that counts something called Inspiration Stump as its most sacred landmark.

Evangeline took her out to the site, a spiritual retreat at the end of a trail in Leolyn Woods. As they hiked over, she explained in a hushed, reverent tone that otherworldly energy is stronger at the stump than anywhere else in Lily Dale.

After that buildup, Calla expected to experience something profound there, as they stood staring at the concrete-encased stump, listening to the soft patter of raindrops. But she felt nothing other than slightly chilled and damp. Evangeline, who was hoping to run into Jacy there, seemed disappointed both in Calla's reaction and Jacy's absence.

On the way back to Cottage Row, Evangeline confessed that she has a major crush on Jacy. Surprise, surprise. "Does he like you, too?" Calla asked cautiously, telling herself that she couldn't be interested in Jacy now. Not if she wanted to keep Evangeline as a friend—and she did.

"He's so quiet it's hard to tell how he feels. About anything. I wish you could meet him."

Calla hesitated before saying, "I'm sure I will." *Why didn't you tell her you already did?* Maybe because she felt guilty, having been instantly attracted to Evangeline's crush.

Evangeline invited her to come to a message circle—a regular gathering of mediums and visitors hoping to receive communication from lost loved ones.

"Jacy always goes," she said, "and Blue, too. Pretty much everyone goes."

Blue. Okay, that's one good reason to show up there. Evangeline doesn't seem interested in him. Just a little awed.

"Is Jacy a medium, too?" she asked Evangeline.

"He's definitely gifted . . . he's in tune with nature and animals. But he hasn't said much about it—about anything, really. Not to me, anyway. Not that he talks to anyone else, either."

"How many kids our age are there in Lily Dale?" Calla asked, noticing she hadn't seen many in their travels.

"Maybe a dozen."

Calla's jaw dropped. "That's it?"

"Within the gates, that's it. Remember, hardly anyone lives here year-round, and a lot of the mediums are single, or older, so . . ." She shrugged.

"Where's your school?" Calla asked, picturing one of

those one-room deals, like they had a hundred years ago. "Is it here in town?"

"No, about a mile away. It's a centralized district. There are other kids who live on farms around here, and they go to school with us."

Now, as Calla settles onto her bed with the books, listening to the rain pinging against the gutter above her window, she decides there are worse places to be.

In the house where your mom just died is at the top of the list. Under the same roof with your ex-boyfriend and his new girlfriend ranks not far beneath it.

I might as well be here in Lily Dale for now, she thinks, opening the first book. *And I might as well find out as much about it— and this thing called spiritualism—as I can.*

Restless, Calla sets aside yet another of the books she took out of the library. This time, she couldn't get past the third page.

She sets it on top of the stack with the other unread titles and vows to get back to them later today—or, preferably, some other day. Not that she finds local history dull, but she isn't in the mood to start at the beginning, with the town's nineteenth-century origins at the dawning of the spiritualist movement, fueled by the Fox sisters' so-called spirit rappings up in Hydesville.

Intriguing, yes . . . but at the moment, she's much more interested in the town's more recent history—say, when her mother lived here.

She gets off the bed and glances at the window, where

a steady rain is still falling outside. Oops—it's blowing in through the cracked window, spattering the sill and the floor with droplets.

She hurriedly yanks it shut and wipes up the moisture with her sleeve.

It already feels stuffy in here, she thinks, as she crosses the room to the dresser. But she knows water isn't good for wood. Mom was a stickler about wiping things up.

And she wouldn't be thrilled to see me using my sleeve to do it, Calla thinks ruefully.

With a sigh, she picks up the nearest picture frame. In this particular snapshot, Mom—with impossibly tall, gravity-defying hair—is wearing a satiny gown and a wrist corsage. She's posing with some guy in an equally pouffy mullet. Calla smiles at the outdated styles and wonders who he is. An old boyfriend of Mom's, obviously.

She never mentioned anyone by name, but when she was trying to comfort Calla over the breakup with Kevin, she did hint at having had her own heart broken once. Calla started to ask for details but her father came in right then, and she got the sense that her mother didn't want to talk about it in front of him.

Or maybe Mom didn't want to talk about it at all, she reflects now, looking back. There was definitely something awkward in her mother's expression even before Dad popped up.

Maybe that was simply because Stephanie rarely brought up the past—her own, and in general. Nostalgia just wasn't her style.

No remember-whens or what-ifs for Stephanie Delaney. She lived in the present.

So did Calla, until recently. Now, she finds herself clinging to the past—her own, her mother's, the past in general. Which is probably because the present is too damned painful.

She frowns, staring at the picture of Mom in her youth, so focused on the striking resemblance between herself and her mom that it takes her some time to notice the nagging thought making its way into her brain: there's something familiar about the boy in the picture. Definitely.

I've seen him before, Calla decides, and wonders how that's possible. She's never been here before . . . and no one from Lily Dale, other than Odelia, has ever visited Mom in Florida.

Okay, so maybe she's mistaken about the boy's being familiar. She looks more closely at the picture. Maybe he just reminds her of someone she knows from school or something.

With a sigh, she sets the picture back among the other frames. She isn't in the mood to see her mother with strangers she can't identify.

It seems almost like a betrayal that Mom lived this whole life she knows nothing about.

Come on, Calla. You know that's not fair. Every adult has a youth their children weren't a part of. That's just how it is.

Yes, but some parents love to talk about their past. Like Mrs. Wilson; she's always bringing up the old days. Lisa hangs on every word, but it used to bug Kevin when his mother went on and on about being a debutante up in Savannah or a sorority girl in Alabama.

At least if Mom were still around, Calla could ask her about her life here in the Dale and the people she knew here. She feels cheated—and puzzled.

Her mother went out of her way to keep a key part of her past hidden. Why?

Why didn't you tell us that your mother was a psychic, or that you lived in a town filled with them? Were you that ashamed of it, Mom?

Probably, knowing her.

With a sigh, Calla turns away from the old photos. Her gaze falls on the clock.

It's still flashing 12:00.

I should set it, she thinks—then remembers that she can't. Not without knowing the correct time, and she doesn't. Her watch is back in Florida with the other stuff she forgot.

I should have made a list before I packed. Mom would have done that. She wouldn't have forgotten anything.

All right, so setting the clock can wait.

Now what?

Odelia is downstairs making banana bread. *I can go help her*, Calla thinks, but quickly vetoes that idea. She isn't in the mood to talk to anyone.

Well, not to her grandmother, anyway. She'd give anything to be able to pick up the phone and call Lisa right now, but she can't do that with Odelia in earshot.

I can go next door and e-mail her.

But then she'd have to talk to Evangeline again, and she isn't in the mood—though she really would love to get in touch with Lisa.

Okay. So I can listen to music or read.

She finds herself looking past her iPod and the stack of library books, though, to the jewelry box that once belonged to her mother.

Walking over to it, she can feel her heart beating in

anticipation. She reaches out to open the lid, and is surprised when the haunting little melody promptly fills the room.

That's odd.

It wound all the way down to silence yesterday when she was here with Odelia. How can it play now without somebody having turned the key again?

Maybe Odelia came back in and did that? Then again, she seemed just as surprised yesterday to hear the music playing—and she didn't seem to find the tune familiar.

Not like I do.

Struck, once again, by the distinct sense that she's heard this song before, Calla listens intently and tries to figure out where.

As the song winds down, she comes up with nothing at all. Well, maybe she's mistaken, just like with the picture of Mom's old boyfr—

She gasps aloud, startled by a glimmer of realization. But it flits into and out of her head before she can catch it.

Something about the song. And the boy in the picture.

What does one have to do with the other, though? Calla bites her lip, trying desperately to grab the elusive thought fragment, but it refuses to land.

Frustrated, she browses idly through the contents of the box: a couple of bead necklaces, fake pearls, several pairs of earrings, some bangles. She examines a little gold angel-shaped pin and a mother-of-pearl ring, trying it on and finding it a perfect fit. She takes it off again, though. It doesn't feel right to wear jewelry her mother didn't actually give to her, as she did the emerald bracelet. Not yet, anyway. Maybe someday.

She shivers and closes the box, restless.

Gradually, she becomes aware of a faint perfume that seems to waft in the room. Sniffing the air, she notices that it's decidedly floral . . . and recognizable.

It's the same thing she smelled out on the porch the other day when she first got here. Some flowers in Odelia's garden must be so strongly scented that the fragrance drifted in the open window and lingered even after Calla closed it. *But why didn't I notice it till now?*

She remembers the sweet aroma of baking banana bread earlier—but not flowers.

She takes another deep breath, and somehow, the floral fragrance seems to be gone. She smells only banana bread now.

Maybe she just imagined the flowers? What other explanation is there?

She didn't imagine the music-box song, though. There's something familiar about it.

And about the boy in the picture.

And I have no idea why, Calla thinks, rubbing her temples furiously in frustration.

Then she realizes, with a start, that it seems to be growing colder in the room.

But I just closed the window. And it was stuffy in here, she remembers.

She shivers, hugging herself in the chill, and crosses over to the window again, wondering if a patch of cool, floral-scented air were somehow trapped inside, even as she tells herself that the idea makes no sense whatsoever.

She gives the bottom of the sash an upward tug. It doesn't budge.

Odelia mentioned that the old windows stick when it's warm and damp out.

Only, it isn't warm in here at all now. It's so not warm, in fact, that Calla is surprised she can't actually see her breath, which is coming quickly now as panic begins to build inside her.

The air smells like flowers again. Oh, God. She's starting to hyperventilate.

Don't freak out. Everything is okay. You're letting your imagination get carried away.

Only the cold isn't her imagination.

Nor is the distinct scent of flowers.

Nor, she realizes with a stab of foreboding, is the pale face staring at her from the other side of the second-story windowpane.

NINE

It's *her*.

The woman Calla saw in the cemetery. And she appears to be floating in midair just beyond the bedroom window. For a moment, Calla is so shocked—and terrified—that all she can do is stand and stare.

Then a frantic scream erupts from somewhere, and it takes her a moment to realize that it came from her.

Immediately, she hears pounding footsteps on the stairs, and Odelia's voice calling, "Calla? Are you okay?"

She can't answer. Before her stunned eyes, the woman's face just disappeared.

"Calla!" Odelia bursts into the room. "What's wrong? Did you see a mouse?"

"What? No, I—" Seeing the sudden, knowing look in her grandmother's eye, Calla clamps her mouth shut. She doesn't dare tell Odelia that she just saw . . . a ghost?

If she tells her grandmother, she'll be instantly pegged as one of "them."

And I can't handle that now, on top of everything else. It was my imagination. That's all it was. Just my imagination. It has to be.

"Calla?" Odelia is waiting expectantly.

"Yeah," she says slowly, backing away from the window. "I did. I saw a mouse."

"Where?"

"Right there," she points vaguely.

"Out the window?" Odelia sounds dubious.

She doesn't believe me. I have to make her believe me. I can't let her know what really happened.

"No, it was here in the room . . . on, uh, the windowsill." She shudders. "I hate mice." That much, at least, is true.

"I've had a problem with mice before, but not at this time of year. Where did it go?"

"I don't know. . . . I screamed and she disappeared."

"She?" Odelia looks amused.

"I mean *he*. Or *it*."

Calm down, Calla warns herself, *before you blab everything to her, and she gets you a shingle of your own to hang over her porch.*

Somewhere in the back of her shell-shocked mind, though, she knows her grandmother's reaction should be the least of her worries if she really has started seeing dead people.

What does it mean? Is she a medium? A psychic?

It's not women's intuition at all, is it? It's . . . what did Evangeline say?

Clairvoyance. That's it. The mere word brings mental images of creepy, vacant-eyed prophets you see in horror movies.

127

Okay, you're blowing this whole thing way out of proportion, she tells herself.

"You know," Odelia is saying, "my friend Andy mentioned the other day that his cat had just had kittens, and he asked if I wanted one."

Blowing what out of proportion? Some creepy woman floating in midair, then disappearing? How can you blow that out of proportion? It's—huge. That's what it is. Huge. And scary.

It was definitely cold in here, too, and there was an intense floral scent just before she saw the woman. For no apparent reason. The window was closed. And what about the music box? And the clock?

"I said no . . . but maybe I should reconsider," Odelia muses. "What do you think?"

"Hmm?" Calla asks absently, her thoughts skittering as wildly about her head as her heart is in her ribcage.

"The cat . . . to catch the mice. Should we get one?"

We? Calla shrugs, carefully avoiding both Odelia's gaze and the window, afraid of what she might see in either. Gone is her eagerness to feel like a part of her grandmother's household, and her mother's hometown.

There is no longer a *we*, as far as she's concerned. She's out of here. No way is she staying in Lily Dale till September. Being here among the spiritualists—and the spirit world—seems to have opened some kind of . . . of . . . personal paranormal portal.

No, she's leaving, definitely . . . just as soon as she figures out where she can possibly go.

"I'll take two scoops of cookies-and-cream in a sugar cone," Calla tells the girl at the snack window at the outdoor café, located beneath a large gazebo. Beyond its perimeter, a soft summer rain is falling.

Calla looks at Evangeline. "What are you having? My treat."

"Oh, that's all right. I've got it."

"Let me treat you," Calla insists. "After all, I dragged you out in the rain." When she glanced out Odelia's living room window and spotted Evangeline reading a book on her front porch a little while ago, her spirits soared. She'd spent a lonely morning watching TV and moping around. By lunchtime, she was not only homesick, she was stir-crazy.

"It's not like I had anything better to do," Evangeline replies with a smile. "I'll have one scoop of chocolate, even though I shouldn't. I'm on a diet. But I guess if this is all I eat for lunch, it isn't so bad."

"You're always on a diet, Evangeline." The girl behind the counter hands Calla her cone.

"Yeah, only I never lose weight. Gee, I wonder why? Think it's because I'm a regular here?" Evangeline shakes her head ruefully. "Oh, hey, Calla, this is Lena. She's a year behind me in school. Lena, Calla."

"Odelia's granddaughter, right? From down south?"

"Word's out already about the new girl in town, huh?" Evangeline asks as Lena begins scooping ice cream from the cardboard tub of chocolate.

"Yeah, Willow said something about it when she was down here this morning."

Willow? Calla can't help but wonder who that is, and why she's talking about her.

"Yeah, I'll just bet she did." Evangeline smirks.

"Who's—" Calla begins, but her question is cut short by Lena.

"Look who's here," the girl mutters.

Calla turns to see Blue Slayton sauntering up to the window, hands in the pockets of his khaki shorts.

Thank goodness she took the time to change out of the sloppy sweats she'd worn all morning. The cutoffs, T-shirt, and sandals she has on now aren't exactly her best outfit, but they're more flattering than baggy cotton fleece. She's not wearing makeup, but at least her long hair is down, and recently brushed, if a little damp from the rain.

"Hey, are you following me around, or what?" Blue asks Calla good-naturedly.

"I got here first, so it's more like the other way around, don't you think?" She takes a demure lick of her ice cream cone, wondering how she's managing to come across as so laid-back when her heart is beating wildly at the sight of him.

"You caught me," Blue returns easily. He barely flicks a glance in the direction of the other two girls as he says, "Hey, Evangeline. Hi, Lena."

"What's up, Blue?" Evangeline asks as Calla pays for their two cones. "Is your dad around? My aunt needed to talk to him about something."

"Nah, he's in L.A. till next week. I'll take a large coffee," he tells Lena, without missing a beat. "Black. Two sugars."

Then, to Calla, "What have you been doing with yourself since you got here?"

Trying to figure out how to get out of here, mostly, she

thinks heavily. To Blue, she says only, "Just hanging out. You know."

"Yeah. Not much else to do around here." He shrugs. "You still want to hook up sometime?"

"Sure."

"Good." He nods.

When? Calla wants to ask, but doesn't.

And he doesn't say anything else, other than to tell her he'll see her around.

As he strolls away with his coffee, Calla and Evangeline slip into seats at a table with their ice cream.

The moment Blue is out of earshot, Evangeline says, "I knew it. I told you he liked you."

"It's not like he asked me out."

"He said he's going to."

Calla shrugs and licks her cone, trying to act as though she doesn't care either way. "He'd better hurry up," she says, "because it's not like I'm here forever."

"Want me to nudge him?"

"No!"

Evangeline laughs. "Okay, okay, I won't say anything. I'm sure he'll get around to it on his own. I just wish Jacy would look at me the way Blue just looked at you," she adds wistfully.

"Maybe you should make the first move," Calla suggests. "You said he's shy, right?"

"Yeah. Really shy. You'll see. I really can't believe you haven't met him yet. This is as small as small towns get."

"Yeah. I'm starting to figure that out," Calla murmurs,

again feeling guilty for not having told Evangeline she and Jacy have already been introduced.

"You'll get used to it."

I don't think I'll have time, Calla thinks, but she doesn't say that to Evangeline. She hasn't given up the idea of leaving Lily Dale as soon as possible. She just hasn't come up with a plan yet.

In the middle of the afternoon, her father calls.

"What are you doing?" he asks, and Calla wonders fleetingly if she should tell him the truth: that she was just lying on Odelia's couch, reading a book about the origins of spiritualism.

"Reading," she says briefly, and waits for him to ask what she was reading. That will open the door to a conversation about Lily Dale, and put the wheels in motion to get her out of here.

That's what she wants, right?

Right. Definitely. It's what I want.

But her father doesn't ask what she is reading, and for some reason, Calla finds herself changing the subject.

"Guess what? I went out for ice cream today with a girl who lives here. She's my age."

"You don't know how happy I am to hear that. I've been thinking you must be lonely with just your grandmother for company. I was even wondering if you'd be able to stick it out there for the whole three weeks, so . . . I'm glad you found a friend. What's her name?"

"Evangeline Taggart," Calla murmurs, wishing he hadn't

just said all that. He's obviously relieved, thinking he doesn't have to worry about her for the time being.

How can she ask him to get her out of here on the heels of this conversation?

You can't. You'll just have to stick it out, like he said.

"Evangeline, huh? That's an odd name."

Speaking of odd, Dad, she's a medium. And so is Odelia. And everyone else in town.

"She lives right there in Lily Dale?" he's asking.

"Right next door." *With her aunt. Also a medium.*

"Well, that's convenient."

"Yeah." She clears her throat. "What have you been doing, Dad?"

"Apartment hunting. Familiarizing myself with the campus. Getting organized for the semester. Going to meetings." There's a pause. "Missing you. And . . . Mom."

The last word is spoken so softly Calla has to strain to hear it.

"I miss her, too, Dad. So much. And I miss you." Her voice breaks, and she swipes at tears in her eyes.

"Well, it won't be long before you're here in California with me," he says hoarsely.

"Yeah. That'll be good."

No, it won't. That's not what she wants—to be with him in a strange place, without Mom or Odelia—

Odelia? Huh?

That's really strange. Why was she feeling, for a moment there, as though she needed to be with her grandmother? She's gone over a decade without Odelia in her life. Sure, Odelia's popped back into it now, but that doesn't mean she's there to stay.

133

Funny, though . . . when she thinks about leaving her grandmother and Lily Dale behind come September, she feels a sad little pang.

Yes, she'll definitely stick it out until then.

She might even miss it when she's gone, she dares to think—and then pushes the thought away.

TEN

"You must be Calla." The woman smiling from the other side of the screen door is attractive, in a bohemian way. Long, curly brown hair, dangling earrings, a jean jacket, and a flowing skirt that brushes her ankles.

"I'm Evangeline's aunt Ramona," she adds unnecessarily.

Right. Calla glances at the sign. She's RAMONA TAGGART, REGISTERED MEDIUM, to be more specific.

"It's nice to meet you."

"You, too."

"Is Evangeline here? I guess I'm a little early. . . . We're supposed to hang out this afternoon." *And I want to use your computer.*

"She mentioned you'd be popping over. She should be back soon. Come on in and wait."

"Thanks." Calla steps over the threshold and hands Ramona

a foil-wrapped loaf. "This is from my grandmother. She made it yesterday."

"Banana bread?"

"How'd you know?"

How do you think she knows? Calla asks herself, instantly irritated by her own question. *She's a medium, isn't she? All mediums are psychic.*

Ramona merely says, however, in response to Calla's inquiry, "That's Odelia's specialty. Whenever anyone in the Dale has overripe bananas, they send them her way and she sends back a loaf of banana bread. I never send bananas over—my nephew the bottomless pit eats them all before they get too ripe—but she sends us bread, anyway. She's some cook, huh?"

She nods politely. Her grandmother is pretty good in the kitchen. But Calla honestly hasn't paid much attention to their meals lately, with everything else that's been going on. She's been preoccupied by the creepy events around here, not to mention exhausted. She didn't sleep very well last night, to say the least.

She'd had that dream again, about her mother and grandmother fighting. It woke her up . . . at exactly 3:17. Again.

There are no coincidences. She read that line in one of the Lily Dale books from the library last night, and it's stuck with her. So has an unsettling chapter about spirits disrupting electronic devices.

Today, the clock is back to flashing 12:00. How can that be, if it was showing the right time in the middle of the night? When Calla asked Odelia, she said she hadn't touched it. Even if she were lying about that a second time—*why would she be?*—Calla figures the clock would have held the time all along. It wouldn't have shown 3:17 in the wee hours and gone back to flashing after sun-up.

"Want to come into the den," Ramona asks, "and talk to me while I paint?"

"Okay." Calla wishes she could get up the nerve to ask if she can check her e-mail.

"So, Evangeline told me she showed you around," Ramona tells her, leading the way into the house. Calla wonders if she also mentioned to her aunt that Calla was hoping to use their computer. Ramona doesn't mention it, saying only, "What do you think of the Dale?"

"It's really nice," Calla says lamely. "So . . . where did Evangeline go?"

"What's today, Friday?"

"Thursday."

"Thursday. That's Crystal Healing, I think."

"Crystal Healing?"

"Evangeline's Thursday class," Ramona explains, as though that answers any question Calla could possibly have.

Back home, sixteen-year-old girls take gymnastics lessons after school, Calla wants to say, but doesn't. She follows Ramona through a living room very much like her grandmother's next door, from the hardwood and antique moldings to the clutter everywhere. Housekeeping doesn't appear to be Ramona Taggart's strong suit any more than it is Odelia's.

At least she's painting, though, Calla tells herself as Ramona opens the door to a room off the equally cluttered dining room. Odelia's shabby rooms could use a paint job as well. But she can't quite envision her grandmother in coveralls with a roller in hand.

Come to think of it, Ramona isn't wearing coveralls, either, and there isn't a roller or paint tray in sight when they step into the den.

What's there is a computer. But it's not even turned on, and Calla doesn't feel comfortable asking about it. There's also an easel. It's set up in one corner, in a rectangle of rare afternoon sunlight falling through the back window.

Oh. So she's not painting the room. She's painting . . . the garden?

Stepping closer to the easel, Calla sees a half-finished outdoor scene that mirrors the view beyond the window. Sort of. There's a bedraggled patch of sunflowers out there, and they're in the painting. Sort of. There are stick-straight, towering green stalks and yellow-brown blobs, anyway. That tall black thing is probably the tree by the back fence, and the little white splotch must be the birdhouse hanging from its branch.

"What do you think?" Ramona asks, coming up behind Calla to survey her own work, palette in hand. "I took some art lessons last winter."

So, paranormal studies aren't the only kind offered around here. That's encouraging, Calla thinks, as she tells Ramona, "I don't know much about painting, but it's pretty good."

"You're right, you don't know much about painting . . . it's awful." Ramona laughs.

"I don't think it's awful." Not *that* awful, anyway.

"Sure it is. But I can't help it. It's so windy around here, everything keeps moving around all the time. And I can't get

138

the light right. It's never consistent. Just when I think I've got it, the sun will go behind a cloud, or it will suddenly burst through on a cloudy day. The weather here is just so unpredictable, you know?"

Calla nods vehemently. She can't seem to get a handle on how to dress. She'll put on a sweatshirt and jacket only to strip them off layer by layer when it starts to feel muggy. Or she'll wake up in a warm room and put shorts on, and by afternoon a cold wind covers her bare limbs in goose bumps.

If only the wind were the only thing around here that brings on goose bumps.

"I never should have tried to show the flowers standing straight and tall that way," Ramona is saying, studying her artwork. "I should have just stuck with them the way they are. Droopy. They don't look real the way I painted them, do they?"

"Not really," Calla confesses, sensing that Ramona wants an honest opinion.

"There you go . . . now you're being straightforward. Just like your mom," Ramona adds with a laugh, catching Calla completely off guard. "She always shot straight from the hip. That was one of the great things about her."

"My mom?" she echoes.

Of course! Of course Ramona would have known Mom. Evangeline mentioned that her aunt grew up in this house. Why hadn't Calla thought of her before?

Because you hadn't even met her, that's why. Now that she has . . .

"Were you and my mom friends?" she asks, trying not to come across as if she's pouncing on Ramona. "When she lived here, I mean. Years ago."

"Oh, Stephanie was a few years older than I was. I have to say, she was always sweet to me," Ramona adds with a fond, faraway smile, picking up the paintbrush again, "even though she thought I was a pain in the—well, you know how it is with pesky little kids hanging around."

Actually, Calla doesn't know how it is. She's an only child, and none of her geriatric neighbors back home in Florida have kids. Not kids who are younger than Calla, anyway. Or younger than thirty, for that matter.

"No, I don't know how it is, but I can imagine," she murmurs, trying to picture Ramona Taggart as a pesky pain to a teenage Stephanie's butt.

"My brother Shawn—he was Evangeline's dad—was a few years older than Steph, and I think he thought of her the same way she thought of me," Ramona goes on with a sad smile. "I still haven't gotten used to his being gone, you know . . . and now, there's no way I can grasp that Stephanie is, too. The last time I saw her, she was about your age—and she looked just like you, by the way. Did anyone ever tell you that?"

"Lots of people have," Calla admits as Ramona dabs at the canvas with the brush, "but no one who knew her when she was actually my age."

"Well, I did. And you could *be* her at . . . how old are you? Seventeen?"

"Yes. Did she have . . . a boyfriend? Back then?" She tries to keep the question casual, though she holds her breath for the reply.

"She had quite a few, from what I remember. She was beautiful, and fun, and—just the kind of person everyone wanted to be around. You know what I mean?"

Calla nods, suddenly missing her mother. Desperately. She feels a fresh wave of grief coming over her. She turns toward the window, trying not to blink and let the tears spill over.

"Calla . . . I'm sorry. I didn't mean to upset you. I know what it's like to lose a mother. I lost mine a few years ago."

At least you had her until you were grown up.

"Evangeline knows, too," Ramona adds softly.

At least she was too little to know what was happening at the time, Calla finds herself thinking, no longer empathetic toward Evangeline for being orphaned so young. *She said she doesn't even remember the accident. At least she isn't stuck with this horrible gory image that will haunt her for the rest of her life.*

Never in her life has Calla felt so utterly alone.

You feel like nobody has ever been in your shoes before, don't you? Nobody's heart has ever been broken this badly before.

That's her mother's voice, echoing in her head.

Those are things her mother said when Kevin dumped Calla, just a few months ago. She could have been referring to how Calla's feeling now, though.

Listen, other people have gone through this, and worse, Calla. They've survived. And you'll survive. No matter how bad it gets, no matter how alone you feel, you'll get through it. I promise you. And I'll always be here for you.

Her voice choked with a sob, Calla manages to say, as she pushes past Ramona, "Can you . . . can you tell Evangeline I couldn't stay?"

"Sure, but . . . are you—?"

"I just . . . I need . . . to go home. I'm sorry."

With that, she runs from the house. Outside, though, she falters at the foot of the steps. A cool breeze whispers in the boughs overhead. Calla looks up, blinded by the sun and her tears.

I need to go home.

But Odelia's house isn't home. Lily Dale isn't home. Even Tampa isn't home anymore.

She squeezes her eyes shut, hot tears spilling down her cheeks.

Mom . . . help me, Mommy. Where do I go? What do I do? I'm so lost.

She spins around blindly, opens her eyes again . . . and finds herself looking at the lake.

Standing on the grassy shore, in the distance, she can clearly see the outline of a woman in the glare of the sun.

ELEVEN

Calla takes off running toward the lake, her eyes fastened on the woman standing beside the shimmering water. She doesn't dare look away.

The person is too distant for Calla to make out more than her silhouette—she's wearing some kind of long dress or robe—but there's something about her that seems to beckon.

Mom! Is that you?

Calla's sneaker hits a rough patch of pavement and she lurches forward. She looks down, sees that it's a pothole—the streets here are full of them—and manages to regain her balance.

When she looks up again, her gaze darts ahead, toward the woman.

But she's gone. It's as though she's simply evaporated into thin air.

"No!" Calla cries out. "Wait!"

She picks up speed, hurtling toward the lake, thinking she

might spot the figure off to the side or slipping behind a tree. But when she gets to the grassy, parklike spot beside the lake, there's no one around.

It probably wasn't Mom anyway.

Calla sinks onto a bench overlooking the water. Of course it wasn't Mom. It didn't feel like her, and anyway . . .

Her mother is gone. Forever. Calla is alone.

No matter how bad it gets, no matter how alone you feel, you'll get through it. I promise you. And I'll always be here for you.

"Then where are you now, Mom?" Calla whispers . . . just as a shadow falls across the grass in front of her.

"Excuse me?" a voice says, and she looks up to see Jacy Bly standing there. His glossy hair is spiked on top today, and she has a feeling he didn't gel it to make it spike that way. There's a no-fuss, laid-back aura about him. He's wearing a faded maroon T-shirt and dark jeans that bag around his bare feet, and he's carrying a fishing pole and tackle box.

"Oh . . . hi. I was just talking to . . ." *My dead mother.* Here in Lily Dale, that wouldn't necessarily raise an eyebrow. But Calla finishes the sentence with ". . . myself."

He says nothing, watching her through eyes so dark they're black. They slant a bit at the corners, almost seeming to squint a bit beneath straight slashes of brow. He's got high, pronounced cheekbones and the fullest lips she's ever seen on a boy. On anyone, really.

She drags her gaze away from his lips—and her brain from the crazy thought of kissing them. *Where did that come from?*

"Listen, did you see anyone around here a few minutes ago?" she asks him. "A woman?"

"Around here?"

She nods, gesturing at the spot. "She was standing right over there when I got here, but . . . she left."

"I didn't see anyone."

"I didn't think so," Calla mutters. Jacy just looks at her. "So, you're, uh . . . going fishing?" she asks stupidly. After all, he's holding fishing gear and heading toward a body of water.

He nods.

"Do you fish a lot?"

Another nod. "How about you?"

He's so soft-spoken, she can't help but feel like a blithering idiot.

A loud one, at that. "Me?" she practically shouts at him.

She tones it down with effort, asking in a near whisper, "You mean, do I fish?"

"Yeah."

"No, I live in Florida," she says, to prove that she specializes in moronic comments.

Jeesh, why can't she get it together conversationally? You'd think she'd never spoken to a good-looking guy before.

"Florida . . . so there aren't any fish down south, huh?" Jacy asks quietly, then those full lips of his part into a beautiful, white-toothed smile.

Calla breaks into a grin. "Nope," she says lightly, "no fish at all."

He gestures with his pole. "You want to try?"

"Fishing?" *No, fencing. Idiot.*

"How about it?" he asks.

She hesitates.

Don't say anything stupid, she warns herself. *For God's sake, just say yes.*

And, to her relief—and his, as far as she can tell—she does.

"There you are!" Odelia sticks her head in from the kitchen the moment Calla walks in the door. "Where have you been?"

"I went for a walk," she says, not wanting to get into meeting Jacy. Which definitely took her mind off everything that's been going on lately.

He's the first guy she's hung out with since Kevin. And as much as she tried not to notice how cute he is—well, she couldn't help it. Sitting side by side on the pier, legs dangling over the water, they sat and fished for over an hour. Sometimes they talked, sometimes they didn't—and for some reason, it didn't matter when they didn't.

Calla finds that unusual, because back in the beginning with Kevin, she always got nervous when she ran out of things to say. Not that she's thinking this is any kind of "beginning" with Jacy.

Still . . . back when she and Kevin first started hanging out alone together, without Lisa as a buffer, Calla used to chatter about anything and everything just to avoid awkward silence.

With Jacy, even though he's pretty much a stranger, somehow the silence wasn't awkward. Maybe because that's such an obvious part of his introspective nature.

"Evangeline came over looking for you," Odelia says. "I thought you were over at the Taggarts' all this time, but she said you'd been there and left."

"I just felt funny hanging around with her aunt, waiting

for her." *And now I feel guilty that I was down by the lake with her crush.*

"Ramona is great. I'm surprised you felt uncomfortable with her."

"It wasn't her, really . . . it was . . . I just felt like taking a walk."

"So how was it?" Odelia asks directly, and something in her expression—and her tone—tells Calla that she doesn't buy her story.

Yeah, it's pretty hard to pull one over on a psychic. Poor Mom. What must it have been like for her, growing up?

"It was a good walk," Calla tells her, relieved when Odelia doesn't call her on it.

"Well, you had company while you were gone."

"Evangeline. I know. You said." *And in this town Evangeline will probably hear about my fishing with Jacy—or, who knows, have a vision about it—any second now.*

"No, not just Evangeline. Someone came and brought you these." Odelia lifts a vase filled with wildflowers from a small table near the stairs.

Calla's eyes widen. "Someone brought me flowers? Who was it?"

"Blue Slayton." A smile quirks the edges of Odelia's hot-pink mouth.

Flustered, Calla just stares at the vase. Why would Blue Slayton bring her flowers?

"He said to call him when you got back."

"I . . . uh, I don't have his number."

"Triple five four-seven-eight-two," Odelia recites.

"You have it memorized?"

147

"Honey, this is a tiny town, and everyone here knows everyone else. Plus, Blue's dad and I used to be good friends."

"Used to be?"

Odelia snorts a little. "Back before old Dave went Hollywood."

"Blue's father lives in Hollywood?"

"Not officially. But he spends most of his time in L.A. these days. Psychic to the stars, and all that."

Something tells Calla her grandmother doesn't approve.

"What about Blue? Isn't he in school?"

"Oh, he stays here when his dad's away."

"With his mother?"

"No, the housekeeper. His mother took off a long time ago and she never looked back. Not even for her son."

Odelia sounds bitter. *Oh. She's probably thinking of her ex-husband*, Calla realizes. *He did the same thing to her—and my mom—that Blue's mother did.*

Which also means Blue Slayton can join the sad little motherless club, with her and Evangeline. And Jacy, who told her, in his quiet way while they were fishing, that his parents are both alcoholics. Abusive ones. It wasn't so bad when they lived on the reservation, he said, because he had neighbors who would look out for him. Then his parents moved to an apartment down in Jamestown. It wasn't long before Social Services started showing up, and they finally removed him from his home, which, Jacy added, his parents didn't protest.

He didn't say specifically what his parents did to lose custody of him, and Calla didn't push him to explain. She could tell it was a painful subject for him. She felt privileged that he had shared as much as he did.

"Here you go," Odelia says, and holds out the phone. "You can call Blue."

Still reeling from her breakup with Kevin—oh, all right, mostly from her afternoon with Jacy—she doesn't really feel like talking to another guy.

Then again, she should at least thank Blue for the flowers. It would be rude not to.

She accepts the phone from Odelia. "What did you say his number was?"

Moments later, her grandmother is back in the kitchen, clattering pots and pans, and Blue Slayton is making small talk, then interrupting himself to ask, "You went fishing with Jacy today, huh?"

"How did you know?"

"You can't get away with anything in the Dale," he says casually.

Wow. Did he have a psychic vision of her and Jacy, or what?

"Listen, you want to go out sometime?" Blue asks. "For coffee, or something?"

Coffee? She doesn't drink coffee. But she can hardly say, *How about milk and cookies?*

You could just say no. But that might hurt his feelings. Anyway, Blue Slayton is really cute. As cute as Jacy, in a drastically different way. Plus, it's not like Jacy said anything about seeing her again when they parted ways by the lake. He just waved and said, "See ya."

Yeah, and she was kind of disappointed by that. Despite Evangeline.

"Coffee sometime would be great," she hears herself tell Blue.

He doesn't sound surprised. Thrilled, either. He just says, as though this is all perfectly routine, "Okay, good. So . . . I'll call you."

Oh. He's not going to make a date right now? She almost wishes she'd said no.

Calla hangs up and goes to find her grandmother in the kitchen. Odelia is stirring a bubbling pot on the stove as an old Enya song plays on the countertop radio. Loudly.

Odelia, singing along in an unskilled falsetto, doesn't notice Calla in the doorway.

Calla clears her throat. Odelia doesn't hear her. Calla has to get her attention, but what is she supposed to call her? *Grandma? Odelia?*

So far, she's still managed to avoid conversationally pegging her grandmother with a name. But that can't go on indefinitely. Sooner or later, she's going to have to address her directly. Now is probably a good time to start. *What did I call her when I was a little girl?* Calla wonders, and suddenly, a strange word flits into her head.

"Gammy?" She blurts it without thinking, and Odelia immediately turns her head.

"What did you say?"

"I said . . ." What *did* she say? And why? "I said, uh, 'Grandma'?"

That sounds ridiculously formal for some reason, and Odelia is shaking her head. "No, you said 'Gammy.' I heard you."

"Then why'd you . . ." Calla notices, to her surprise, that her grandmother's eyes are suddenly shiny. ". . . ask?" she finishes, fervently wishing she hadn't said anything at all.

"That's what you used to call me," Odelia says, going back to stirring her soup after swiping a hand at her eyes. "Gammy. When you were a little girl and I used to come see you. But then all those years went by and I thought you must have forgotten."

"I did forget. Until now."

She wants to ask her grandmother why all those years went by without a visit. What did she and Mom disagree about? *I can't ask her yet. Maybe sometime . . . but not now.*

"I'm glad you remembered," her grandmother is saying. "You can still call me that."

"But . . . I'm not a little girl anymore."

Her grandmother waves away her protest. "Call me Gammy. You hear me?"

"Loud and clear." Calla smiles, then remembers why she came into the kitchen in the first place, and her smile fades. "Listen, what time did Blue come over with those flowers?"

"Hmm? Oh, I don't remember, exactly."

"Did he wake you from your nap?" she asks, trying a different tactic, needing to know. "Or before Evangeline came over? Or was it later than that?"

"Oh, it was later. Maybe ten or fifteen minutes before you got home, I guess."

"That late?"

Odelia nods. "Why?"

Because now I know for sure why he brought the flowers over today. It was because he saw me fishing with Jacy Bly, and it bothered him.

That's what she suspected in the first place. Call it intuition, or call it common sense.

It's telling her something else, too: Blue Slayton is the kind of guy who wants what he can't have. If she's interested in him, all she has to do is pretend that she isn't.

But she's never liked to play games, and anyway, she isn't sure she's interested in Blue. Not the way she's interested in Jacy. . . .

Who, she has a feeling, wouldn't be into games, either. But anyway, Evangeline likes him.

Calla sighs. After what happened with Kevin, who needs any of this?

"Calla? It's me!" a familiar voice says over the telephone the following evening.

"Lisa! I'm so glad you called!" And just as glad that Odelia is out at some mediums' league meeting, so she can have a private conversation. "I've been dying to talk to you."

"You too. Listen, I totally get that you don't have access to e-mail—"

Calla opens her mouth to tell her that's about to change.

"But you said you'd call me. Why haven't you?"

Mostly because Kevin might answer the phone, but she doesn't want to admit that. "I feel funny putting long-distance charges on my grandmother's bill. Listen, Lis', I need to talk to you. Things have been kind of crazy here."

"Crazy how? Don't tell me you're seeing ghosts or something!"

She hesitates. She was about to tell her exactly that, but Lisa's tone stops her.

"No, nothing like that," she says slowly. "It's . . . a guy."

Why did she go and say that?

"Two guys, actually," she hears herself say next. *Huh?*

"You're seeing two guys?"

Not really, but it wouldn't hurt to have Lisa mention that to Kevin, would it?

"Yeah," she tells Lisa, feeling only a little guilty. "They're both cute, too . . . so I'm torn."

"Hey, there are worse problems you can have," Lisa says with a laugh.

Yeah, no kidding.

"Listen, Calla, I'm kind of glad you're seeing someone else—two someone elses."

Something in Lisa's tone makes Calla's heart sink. "You're glad? Why?"

"Just . . . It's good you're over Kevin, that's all."

Oh. "You met Annie. And you like her. Right?"

"How'd you know? I mean, I tried not to like her, but she was . . ."

"Likable."

"Lovable. I'm sorry, Calla. I mean, I wish you and my brother would get back together, but since you're not even here—and now you've got two new boyfriends, anyway—well, I hope it's okay with you that I don't hate Annie."

"No, it's fine." Calla paces restlessly across the living room. "I'm glad you like her. I wouldn't want Kevin going out with some loser." *Sure you would.* "Is she still down there?"

"No, she went back." Lisa changes the subject quickly. "Tell me about these two guys!"

Calla does, doing her best to make it sound as though Blue and Jacy are both head over heels about her, and vice versa.

153

"They sound great. Maybe I can help you make up your mind between them," Lisa says. "I asked my parents if I can fly up and visit you before school starts and they didn't say no."

"They said yes?"

"Not exactly. But they're thinking about it. I'll keep you posted."

Calla wonders if it would be a pleasure or a problem to have Lisa visit. A little of both, she decides, after hanging up with a promise to start checking her e-mail at the Taggarts'.

Odelia won't be back for at least another half hour. The house feels eerily empty.

But that's better than eerily not *empty*, Calla reminds herself uneasily.

She read earlier that spirits don't hang around just to give people a good scare. They're usually trying to communicate some kind of message.

Well, whatever it is, I don't want to know. Not when I'm here alone, anyway.

Maybe she should go next door to use the computer right now, even though she just talked to Lisa and her e-mail can wait. Evangeline is probably home. Some company would be nice. And reassuring.

Pausing in front of the window overlooking the street, she glances out to see if there are lights on next door. To her surprise, someone is out there, standing directly in front of Odelia's house, facing it. Watching it.

Feeling exposed, Calla immediately reaches toward the lamp, fumbling for the switch. She finds it and flicks it off, making herself less visible, which, of course, also makes the figure more visible. Calla can see now that it's a female, with long hair.

She's standing just beyond the streetlight's glow, shrouded in shadows.

Calla's skin prickles. Is that the girl from Ohio? The one who was here with her mother?

What's she doing out there now? Why is she staring at Odelia's house?

I should call the police. Calla hurriedly looks around for the telephone receiver she tossed aside earlier. Finding it, she stands poised with it, wondering if 911 works in Lily Dale.

Then she glances out the window again.

The street is empty. The girl is no longer there . . . if she ever was at all.

TWELVE

"Stop it, Mother," Stephanie commanded Odelia. "Just don't say another word about it."

"Stephanie—"

"Stop!" Stephanie glanced down at Calla, who quickly pretended to be focused only on dressing her new doll. "Just drop the whole thing."

"How can I drop it? How can you? Don't you want to know?"

"No, I don't."

"That's unnatural. How can you not—"

"I'm a freak of nature! Is that what you want me to say?"

"Calm down, Stephanie. You're hysterical."

"Well, what do you expect?"

"I expect you to want to know what really happened. And the only way we'll learn the truth is to dredge the lake!"

Calla awakens with a gasp.

The room is dark. Bewildered, she sits up in bed, her pulse racing frantically.

Oh . . . a dream. *That* dream, the one about Mom and Odelia and dredging the lake. She was having it again, after almost an entire week of sleeping soundly.

They were so angry, both Mom and Odelia, flinging things around the room, glaring and pointing fingers at each other.

With a shudder, Calla squeezes her eyes shut to block out the memory. But she can still hear their shrill voices. Is that how it really happened? Is she reliving the scene in her sleep, or creating it in a dream?

She opens her eyes again and her gaze goes automatically to the bedside table, even as she remembers that she never did set the digital clock. It's been flashing all week. . . .

Until now.

Bewildered, she notices the time.

3:17.

With a frustrated cry, she reaches over and yanks the cord out of the socket.

Lying stiffly in bed, wide awake, Calla watches the backdrop beyond the window go from blackish gray to bluish gray to just plain ominous gray as dawn creeps into the room, dark and heavy as a storm cloud.

She's relieved to see nothing but sky out there, yet she can't shake the memory of the face she saw that afternoon not long after she arrived here.

Who are you? Where are you? Are you coming back?

Calla rubs her eyes, knowing she should try to get some sleep if she wants to function at all later. She's never done well on little sleep. A yawn overtakes her, but her body is still clenched and tense. Anyway, it's morning now. Even if she drifts off again, how many hours could she possibly get in?

Her head turns automatically toward the bedside table to check the clock, just as she remembers that she unplugged it in the night.

Or did she? It's flashing 12:00 once again.

Calla jerks upright in bed and grabs the clock. *I know I un-plugged it. I remember!*

She jabs blindly at the buttons on top until the time changes to—and holds at—12:01.

It isn't 12:01. God knows what time it really is. All Calla cares about is that it isn't 3:17.

She slowly returns the clock to the table and stares at it.

She read last week that spirit energy feeds on electronic energy to make its presence known. Meaning, spirits can ma-nipulate appliances and electronic devices—according to the author of the book and his pages upon pages of research sources.

Supposedly, spirits can disrupt a radio signal or even send a certain song that has meaning for someone they left behind.

It stands to reason they can also tamper with a clock.

But if that's the case here, Calla wonders, *what are they trying to tell me with 3:17?*

"Did you find us a place to live yet?" Calla asks her father when he calls that afternoon.

"Not yet. But I'm trying." He says that every day. She's beginning to wonder if he's ever going to find a place for them . . . and what will happen if he doesn't.

"I'm going to see a place by the beach tomorrow," he says optimistically. "It sounds perfect for us, and it's in our price range, and there's a great public school. Cross your fingers."

"I will. But . . . I mean, it's almost September."

"Not yet. We've got plenty of time to find a place."

"I hope so."

"Have you been keeping busy? Hanging around with your new friend Evangeline?"

Surprised her absentminded father remembered the name, Calla says, "A little."

There's a pause. "Is everything okay there, Calla?"

She wonders if she should tell him what's been going on, or pretend everything is fine. In other words, should she stay in Lily Dale another ten days as she's supposed to, or leave right away? If she tells her father the truth, he'll yank her out of there before she can say boo.

And then what? He doesn't even have a place for me to stay in California.

"Dad?" she asks. "What happens if you decide not to do the sabbatical after all? Can you go back to your job in Florida this semester instead?"

"Nope," he says, "can't do that. I have to do the sabbatical. It'll work out fine. Don't worry. Just enjoy the rest of your time there. You'll be here with me before you know it."

That, Calla thinks as she hangs up, *will be a relief.*

Then again, will it really? Once she leaves Lily Dale, she'll be farther away from her mother than ever. And she might never know what's going on in Odelia's haunted house, or what the ghosts are trying to tell her.

"You're going to the message circle after all?" Odelia asks in surprise, about to walk out the door the next night, when Calla walks downstairs in sneakers and a jacket. "I thought you said at dinner that you were too exhausted."

She shrugs, avoiding Odelia's gaze. "I was, but I splashed some cold water on my face and woke myself up." That's all true. What she doesn't say is that she's so exhausted because she had the same dream yet again last night, and it woke her at 3:17 again. She knows, because she saw the clock, which she was certain she'd left unplugged when she went to bed.

Maybe if she gets rid of the clock, the inexplicable, silent 3:17 wake-up call will just go away.

She threw the clock into the kitchen garbage, carrying the bag out to the can behind the shed for good measure. Maybe she can't control her dreams, but she's finished with the clock.

"Well, I'm glad you changed your mind." Odelia opens the front door. "It's about time you saw what goes on here. Come on."

Calla follows her out into the night. "Why don't you ever lock your house?" she asks as Odelia merely pulls the door, and then the screen door, shut behind them.

Calla can't help but think about the girl who was standing out in front of Odelia's house the other night. What did she want? Was she casing the place, planning to rob it or something?

For some reason, she never did mention it to Odelia. Maybe because she's not entirely sure she didn't imagine it.

After all, the girl seemed to be there one minute and gone the next.

At least I know she's real, though, Calla thinks wryly, *since she and her mother were here for a reading that first time.* Yeah, ghosts probably don't need mediums to contact the dead.

"Why would I lock the house?" Odelia asks. "Anything I have in there, people are welcome to take, if they need it that badly. That's one way to clean out clutter, right?"

They head down Cottage Row along the pavement still shiny from today's downpour, which is apparently over—at least, for now. The sky is charcoal colored, not just from the gathering dusk. A lake-blown gust stirs leafy branches over-head, foreshadowing more rain.

"You know, it really is dangerous to leave your house un-locked," Calla persists as they painstakingly make their way toward the auditorium. Odelia, she's noticed, has a hard time moving quickly because of her weight.

"Dangerous? How so?"

"Robbers aren't the only ones who might get in."

"Right. There are mice, too."

"And murderers," Calla says darkly.

"Not around here."

"Murder can happen anywhere."

"Well, I'm not going to worry about that."

"Why not? Because there's no such thing as dying, right? Not really. So what's the worst that can happen if you run into a psycho killer?"

Odelia gives her a long, hard look. "Sure you want to come to this message circle?"

No. But she's going anyway. What better way to top off

another difficult day—for her, anyway. Odelia was contentedly busy giving readings and making a complicated French casserole for dinner, which might have been appealing, if Calla had any appetite.

She didn't, especially after spending the bleak, rainy day alone in her room reading more about Lily Dale. Hours of wading through tedious historic detail and endless spiritualist rhetoric yielded some useful—and, all right, scary—information.

That she's even able to pick up on a spirit's presence at all indicates that Calla, like her grandmother, has a so-called heightened sense of awareness. In other words . . .

Calla seems to be a psychic medium.

A transmitter of sorts, able to bridge the invisible chasm between the living and the dead.

What if all this has something to do with her mother? The first apparition appeared at Mom's grave. The next time was in Mom's girlhood bedroom. And again at the lake.

What if it *is* her mother?

It doesn't look like her—not in the least bit. But what if Mom has taken on some other physical form in the afterlife? That seems as possible as any other far-out theory Calla has come to accept since arriving in Lily Dale.

Then again, the spiritual energy doesn't *feel* like her mother.

No? And what do you know about spiritual energy?

Zilch. Except she would think that if her mother were around, she would feel comforted, not apprehensive.

Operating under the assumption that the spirit in question isn't her mother's but has some connection to her, Calla has to

162

learn to be receptive to whatever it's trying to tell her. Which is why she's going to watch the mediums in action tonight.

"Here we are," her grandmother says, and Calla looks up to see that they've reached the auditorium.

Built in the 1880s, the wooden structure appears as untouched by modern upgrades as any other structure in Lily Dale, inside and out. The large rectangular panels around the perimeter walls have been opened to let in the evening's damp chill. Calla's toes are icy in her sandals, and she wishes she'd put on a sweatshirt under her light jacket. Her thin Florida blood isn't used to these fluctuating temperatures, and she wonders if it ever feels like summer here.

She and Odelia settle into a pair of hard wooden seats in the front of the tiered room, which is slowly beginning to fill. Calla looks around, taking in the polished hardwood floor, the metal poles that stretch to the exposed rafters, the old-fashioned glass-globed light fixtures that hang low among them. Down front is a stage that holds little other than a row of unoccupied chairs to one side and a podium.

Odelia is busily carrying on a gossipy conversation with the middle-aged woman seated on her other side, leaving Calla free to watch people move into their tiered seats. They could be about to see a Broadway show or a concert for all their casual, chatty conversation. You'd never guess from the crowd's overall demeanor that they're here to be put in touch with their dead loved ones—assuming that's why they've all ventured out to this drafty auditorium on a gloomy week-night that feels more like November than August.

Pretty much everyone is casually dressed, including the

mediums who are now taking the stage, settling themselves into the row of chairs there as an expectant hush falls over the room.

Calla can't help but note that all but one of them is female and as plus-sized as her grandmother is, if not more so. The lone exception is a lanky African-American man sitting on the far end of the row.

"Hey, you're here!" a voice whispers somewhere behind Calla, and she feels a tap on her shoulder. Startled, she turns to see Evangeline slipping into a seat behind her.

Calla smiles briefly, first at Evangeline, who returns it, then at the pretty girl sitting with her, who doesn't. Her mouth doesn't even quirk when Evangeline introduces her, still in a whisper. "This is Willow York. She lives here. Willow, this is Odelia's granddaughter, Calla."

"Nice to meet you."

"You, too," Calla murmurs in response, though it doesn't sound like the girl meant it.

Calla doesn't want to feel intimidated by her striking dark hair and eyes, porcelain skin, and delicate bone structure, but it's hard not to. She wishes she had taken the time to at least remove the elastic from her own hair and brush it out, or put on a little makeup to hide her dark under-eye circles. Oh, well. This isn't a beauty pageant, even if Willow York looks as though she should be onstage somewhere other than here, wearing a Miss Something banner.

Wondering if she's always this aloof, or just doesn't like straggly-haired newcomers, Calla turns to face forward again as the session begins with a brief, meditative prayer.

Then the first medium, Debra, comes to the front of the

stage and surveys the audience intently for a moment before seeming to zero in on someone behind Calla to the left.

"I'm back there," Debra announces with a sweep of her hand, "and I have a white-haired man coming through—not gray, but pure white, and he has an awful lot of it. His name is Rod, or Rob, or maybe Bob—something like that. He passed very quickly, either falling from a height, or having something fall from a height onto him—I can't tell which it is."

Hearing a high-pitched gasp, Calla turns to see a woman with short blond hair, covering her mouth with both hands as the man next to her rests a supportive arm around her shoulders.

"Do you know who this is?" the medium asks unnecessarily.

The woman is nodding fiercely. "It's my uncle Roger. We called him Uncle Rodge."

Intrigued, Calla turns back toward Debra, who doesn't look surprised at all.

"He worked at Home Depot," the blond woman goes on, "and he was killed by a pallet of wood or something that fell from a high shelf."

"It's been quite some time, hasn't it?"

"Yes . . . that was almost two years ago. My aunt just got remarried last week."

Debra nods, as if she already knew that. "He wants to tell her that it's okay with him. That he wants her to be happy. He's saying he always told her that she should get on with her life if anything ever happened to him, and that she didn't believe he really meant it. But he did."

"I . . . I don't know if he ever said that." Uncle Rodge's niece is choked with emotion. "I'll ask my aunt."

"Do that. And give her the message, please. It's important."

"I will!" The woman sits down and tilts her temple against that of the man sitting next to her, who whispers something in her ear.

Not sure what to make of what just happened, Calla watches Debra close her eyes as if she's concentrating on something. It could be just an act, she supposes. The medium might have done her homework in advance. An accidental death at Home Depot would probably have made the papers.

But that was two years ago . . . and how would Debra know the victim's niece would be here tonight? Nobody took names at the door. Everyone here is anonymous.

All right, so if Debra didn't research the blond woman in advance, maybe she just made a series of lucky guesses. Lots of elderly men have white—not gray—hair. Some even have a lot of it, though many are balding. And the name—something that sounds like Rob, Rod, or Bob, all fairly common—leaves it pretty open, considering that it could have been interpreted as a first name or a last name or even a nickname. Anyone who lost a white-haired Rob, Rod, or Bob—or anyone with a name remotely similar—at some point in his or her life might have claimed the so-called spirit as his or her own.

Then again, Debra nailed the cause of death. Wouldn't it have been safer for her to guess a heart attack, if she were guessing? Or something even more vague, like "something involving the chest area," which could be a heart attack or cancer or even a blood clot.

Yet Debra chose to be specific: he either fell from a great height or something fell on him. Bingo.

Calla listens with interest as Debra zeroes in on her next message, for a pair of elderly sisters holding hands in the second row. It's from their late mother, who wants them to know that she's doing just fine on the other side, and that there's something wrong with the car one of them drives.

"She's saying you need to have the tire pressure checked, or the oil—something like that," Debra advises as the sisters exchange worried glances and promise to oblige.

Finally, Debra spends a long time trying to find out who in the audience is connected to the spirit of a teenage boy who died in a car crash. There are initially a number of takers, but the number dwindles as the details of his life and death emerge, until at last there's a young girl who barely knew him but was a couple of years behind him at the same school.

"He wants you to get in touch with his mom and tell her it wasn't her fault. He should have been wearing his seat belt. She always told him that, and he didn't listen. He wants her to know that he's okay."

The girl nods, looking upset. "But why would he come to me?"

The medium shrugs. "You never know who you're going to get when you come here. Sometimes the last person you would ever expect to hear from is just waiting to pounce— forgive the expression—because they know you're coming, and they seize the opportunity to get their message delivered to their loved ones using you—and me, for that matter—as the messenger."

The girl seems satisfied with that explanation. Calla is, too . . . which bothers her somewhat.

This is all making so much more sense now, seeing the process in action. But does that mean that she's actually one of them? That she could, with training, do what they do?

I'd be afraid to see spirits all around me all the time.

Yet that thought is swiftly chased from her mind by another: *I'd be able to help people, the way Debra just did.*

She glances around at the people who just received messages. All seem contented, as opposed to the wary expressions worn by some of their seatmates who are still hoping for a reading.

It's a gift, Calla acknowledges as Debra takes her seat to a smattering of applause.

People come here to Lily Dale searching for some connection to their lost loved ones. She, of all people, can relate to their anguished sorrow and longing. That some of the bereaved seem to find comfort here should give Calla hope. Not just for her own grief, but for her gift—if, indeed, she does have one.

But what about me? What good is this gift if I can't even use it to find Mom?

The next medium steps up quickly to take Debra's place. As she begins questioning a section of audience members on the opposite side of the room, Calla begins to feel as though she's being watched. Her breath catching in her throat, she turns her head slowly, expecting to see, once again, the shadowy figure of the woman who's been haunting her.

Instead, she spots Jacy Bly. He's leaning against the door frame, arms folded, and he doesn't look away when she catches him looking at her. She does, though, feeling her face grow hot. She hasn't run into him since the other day, when they went fishing together.

Then again, it's not like she's spent much time walking around Lily Dale. The weather has been crummy, and she's pretty much been holed up in Odelia's house.

Feeling a jab in her shoulder from behind, she turns to see that Evangeline is motioning with her head in the boy's direction. "That's him."

"What? Who?" she whispers back, pretending to be clueless.

"That's Jacy Bly," Evangeline hisses. "Remember I told you about him?"

"Oh . . . right. We met," she admits at last, and is relieved the moment it's out.

"You did? When?"

"I ran into him at the lake the other day, and he, uh, showed me how to drop a fishing line."

Evangeline looks a little dismayed, but she says only, "What did you think of him?"

"He's so quiet. I don't know . . . he was nice."

"Yeah. He is nice." Evangeline shrugs.

Does she think I'm interested in him? Maybe I should tell her I'm not. Only . . .

Calla slips another glance in his direction and finds him still watching her, as though they're the only two people in the room.

Only maybe I am.

Unnerved, she shifts her attention back to the medium doing the reading—at least, she tries to. Every time she sneaks a look at the doorway, she expects Jacy to be gone, like an apparition that may or may not have been there in the first place. But he's still there. And he keeps catching her looking.

I should stop, Calla thinks, but she can't seem to help herself. Evangeline was right. There's something magnetic about him.

Once, when she hastily shifts her attention away from Jacy, she finds herself looking unexpectedly at another familiar face. It's Elaine Riggs, from Ohio. She doesn't see Calla, though. She's focused on the medium onstage, and she looks hopeful. Calla wonders where her daughter is tonight. Hopefully she's not casing Odelia's house again, especially with the door unlocked.

The next medium, a man named Walter, takes the stage. Calla remembers her conversation with Jacy and realizes he's one of Jacy's foster dads.

Watching him in action is fascinating. He's even more accurate and specific than most of the other mediums were, and he delivers his messages with an air of gentle, sympathetic concern.

"I'm getting something for an Eileen . . . Ellen . . . something like that. It's about a child, but . . . this isn't her name. It's the mother's."

Nobody says anything.

"I'm seeing a red Buckeyes shirt," the medium goes on, and someone calls out immediately. Calla turns to see that Elaine Riggs is standing.

"I'm from Ohio. But my name is Elaine—not Eileen."

The medium pauses, seeming to listen, then asks, "Do you have a daughter?"

A sob escapes the woman as she nods.

"I've got a male spirit here, and he's telling me something about your daughter. He's showing me a white paper shopping bag . . . the kind with handles. Like from a department store . . . do you know what this means?"

"I think so." Elaine's shoulders are shaking with emotion and tears are pouring down her cheeks. Why is she so upset?

Is her daughter really a thief? Calla wonders. A shoplifter

or something? That would explain the shopping bag, she decides, pleased she's getting the hang of how this works.

"Spirit is saying you've been upset about something involving your daughter. He wants you to know he's with you . . . this is *not* your husband, though."

"No, my *ex*-husband is alive."

"I feel like this is an older man. It could be your father."

"Yes. Daddy passed away last year."

No wonder she's so emotional. Calla would be a wreck if her mother popped up here without warning. *I wish she would, though. . . . I so wish she would.*

"He's with you," the medium assures the woman again. "He keeps saying that. He really wants to bring you comfort." He pauses, his eyes closed tightly, like he's meditating. "He's showing me a rock."

"A rock? What . . . what do you mean?"

"It's just . . . a rock." Walter frowns. "And there's a house."

"What kind of house?" Elaine asks, almost sounding panicky. "What does it look like?"

"No, it's . . . not a real house. It's a child's drawing. One dimensional. Door in the middle, two windows, chimney with curly crayon smoke . . ."

"I don't know what that means."

Walter appears lost in the vision, shaking his head slowly. After a minute, Elaine asks, "Is he . . . is he saying anything else? Is he showing you anything else?"

"No. His energy is fading. I'm sorry . . . I'm being pulled over here now." The medium is off to the opposite side of the auditorium, to someone else, leaving Elaine crumpled, disappointed, in her seat.

Calla watches her uneasily. She can't help but wish there were something she herself could do. Or, yes, she almost feels as if there's something she's *supposed* to do. To help Elaine. Which is odd, because she's not even sure why Elaine is here.

When the service is over, Evangeline taps her on the shoulder. "What did you think?"

"I thought it was interesting."

"Yeah, there were some good readings tonight. So listen, I thought you might pop over to check your e-mail. You still can, you know."

"I know . . . and thank you. I'll get there at some point."

"Anytime. And you can stay to hang out with me for a while if you want, too."

"Thanks. Hey, where's your friend going?" Calla asks, noticing Willow York by the door.

Evangeline rolls her eyes. "She said she was meeting Blue."

"Blue?"

"Yeah. I hate to say it, but—well, he and Willow are supposedly broken up, but they keep finding reasons to see a lot of each other anyway."

"*She's* his ex-girlfriend?" Calla asks in dismay, and Evangeline nods.

"Supposedly ex."

"So . . . you mean they might still be together?"

"I think Willow wishes they were."

"You *think*? Aren't you friends with her?"

"Not good friends. I mean, there aren't that many people our age around here, like I said, so we all sort of gravitate together. But I wouldn't say Willow and I are friends. She can be kind of standoffish."

Yeah, no kidding. "So she's still into Blue?"

"Seems like it. How about you?" Evangeline asks with a gleam in her eye.

"No!"

"Well, just so you know? I don't think he's into Willow anymore. *He* broke up with *her*."

Evangeline looks pleased to tell her that, probably hoping to get Calla interested in Blue and distracted from Jacy. Calla is secretly pleased to hear it, too. Why, she has no idea. She's not about to "hook up" with Blue Slayton, as he put it, if he's seeing someone else. If she were interested, though, she'd think twice after seeing the exotically beautiful—and standoffish—Willow. If *she's* Blue's type, Calla's not.

Still . . . he did seem interested. *But that doesn't matter.* She's still on the rebound from Kevin, trying to get over him—and anyway, it's not as if she's staying here in Lily Dale. Nothing could come of hooking up with Blue even if it did happen.

Jacy Bly, either.

"Oops, there's my aunt over there waving at me," Evangeline says. "I've got to go."

Calla follows her gaze to Ramona. Beside her is an adolescent boy who has to be Evangeline's brother. He has the same plain, round face and ruddy coloring, and he's wearing a pair of Harry Potter–style glasses that do nothing for him.

"What are you doing tomorrow?" Evangeline asks over her shoulder. "Maybe I'll come over and we can, I don't know, play a game or watch a movie or something."

"Sure," Calla finds herself saying politely, "that would be fun."

It actually might be, she realizes in surprise. She's getting tired of being alone.

"Great. See you then."

She watches Evangeline walk away—and realizes Jacy is promptly approaching her from the opposite direction, as if he were waiting to catch her alone. Her heart beats a little faster as they lock eyes.

"Hi," she says nervously when he reaches her side. There's something about him that unnerves her. Something other than the fact that he's so good-looking. There's a quiet but intense energy about him, and she feels almost helplessly drawn to it. She can't help but remember the energy that zapped her arm the day he shook her hand, and wonders what to make of it.

"This is the first time I've seen you here."

"Probably because it's the first time I've been here." Her flippant comment feels wrong.

"What did you think?"

"I think this auditorium could use some new seats, with cushions," she says wryly, but he doesn't crack a smile.

Great. This is just how things began the first time she spoke to him, by the lake. They hit their conversational stride only when they were fishing and she stopped trying to flirt.

"Seriously?" she adds. "I thought it was fascinating. Is this how it goes every time?"

"Pretty much. Were you hoping for a message?"

That question—and his straightforward gaze—catches her off guard. "What do you mean?"

He shrugs. "Maybe I'm wrong. I thought you hoped your mother would come through."

He isn't wrong. She did hope that. But how did he know?

"Calla?" She looks up to see Odelia beckoning to her from where she's standing with a couple of friends. "Come here. I want you to meet some people."

"I'll see you," Jacy says, and slips away without another word or glance.

Odelia introduces her to Debra, the medium, and to another woman, and to a man named Andy Brighton, whose name Calla recognizes from one of the shingles in town. She carries on polite small talk with them, watching Jacy head for the door with Walter.

The two women leave but Odelia lingers, chatting with Andy about the Medium's League meeting. They discuss it as if it's a bridge club.

"Oh, before I forget, I know you wanted to get the kitten this week, but she's still too young to be taken away from her mother."

"That's okay," Odelia says. "I haven't seen any mice . . . yet. But I'm sure they're there."

A chilling memory stirs back to life in Calla's head. Who was the woman hovering outside the window that day? Should she have confessed the truth to Odelia, instead of making up that stupid story about having seen a mouse? Now her grandmother's getting a cat because of it, she thinks guiltily—though she has to admit Odelia seems enthusiastic as Andy describes the adorable little bundle of fur she can bring home in a few weeks. By then, Calla will be gone anyway.

At last, Andy excuses himself and they're free to leave. Darkness has fallen outside, but it hasn't started raining again.

As they head around the auditorium toward Cottage Row, Calla catches sight of the lake waters gleaming in the glow of a distant lamppost.

The only way we'll learn the truth is to dredge the lake.

"Do you spend much time down there by the water?" she hears herself asking Odelia.

"No," Odelia's answer is prompt, and so resolute that Calla knows instantly that she didn't imagine the conversation between her grandmother and her mother.

Their falling out had something to do with the lake. Dredging the lake, to be specific.

Why do you dredge a lake in the first place? Calla asks herself, and the answer sends a chill slithering down her spine. *You dredge it to bring something—or someone—up from the bottom.*

"Why not?" she persists, hoping to spur her grandmother into spilling whatever it is that she's hiding. "If I were you, I'd hang out by the lake. It's so pretty."

"It's dangerous," Odelia says ominously, quickening her footsteps as much as she's able.

"Why is it dangerous? It's not like you have alligators up here like we do in Florida."

"No, but the current is stronger than you'd think for a lake this size. It pulls people out and under even if they're strong swimmers."

Is that it? Did someone drown here? But what would that have to do with Calla's mother? Why would she have been arguing so violently about it with Odelia that they never spoke again?

"Did my mom like to swim in the lake when she was a kid?" Calla asks.

Odelia's answer is brief. "Sometimes. Listen, I don't want you in the water here, okay?"

"But why not? I'm a good swimmer."

"Just *don't go into that lake*. Do you understand me?"

"Yes." Calla's voice sounds almost meek in the wake of the inexplicable warning.

What on earth happened out there?

She gazes at the still water in the distance, wondering what secrets it might hold in its murky depths, and whether she'll ever find out.

THIRTEEN

A few days later, Calla is putting away the Trivial Pursuit board in the living room when she hears a knock on the front door.

Glancing out the window, she sees a blue BMW parked at the curb. It's a convertible and the top is down on this rare, gorgeous summer afternoon.

It occurs to her that this is the first upscale car she's seen around Lily Dale, and it's hard to imagine it parked in front of one of these worn little lakeside cottages. Must belong to a visitor hoping for a walk-in appointment with Odelia. *Well, you're out of luck*, Calla thinks, heading into the foyer. Her grandmother just started a reading with a regular client, a widow who always books a double appointment.

But it isn't a walk-in after all. Blue Slayton is standing on the porch.

Calla's hand immediately goes to her hair, which is pulled back in a no-frills ponytail. She's wearing cutoffs, a tank top, and flip-flops.

"Hey, how've you been?" Not waiting for an answer, he adds, "Want to go for a ride?"

Calla hesitates. "I'm not really dressed to go out."

"You look good to me." His eyes flick over her, and she's suddenly conscious that her tank top is pretty skimpy. "Come on, it's a gorgeous day. We can get ice cream."

Ice cream is better than coffee, and it is a gorgeous day. It would be nice to ride around with Blue in the sunshine.

"Is that your car?" she asks him, gesturing at the convertible.

"No. It's the maid's." He grins at her shocked expression. "Yeah, it's mine. Come on."

"Okay," she decides impulsively. "Just let me leave a note for my grandmother."

He's already behind the wheel, engine running, when Calla gets to the car, but he jumps out and opens the door for her politely.

"Thanks," she murmurs, slipping past him into the sun-warmed leather passenger's seat. He's so close she can smell the clean cotton scent of the blue T-shirt that exactly matches the shade of his eyes.

Okay, don't go falling for him, she warns herself. *He's a player. That's obvious.*

Blue steers through the narrow streets until they reach the entrance gate again. Seeing it for the first time since her arrival, Calla admires the charming arched grillwork LILY DALE ASSEMBLY sign overhead.

Then she notices the one beneath it that reads: LILY DALE ASSEMBLY . . . WORLD'S LARGEST CENTER FOR THE RELIGION OF SPIRITUALISM.

She missed that one, somehow, on the first day. If she had seen it, she would have been a little more prepared for what met her within the gates.

Funny what she's quickly learned to take in stride. She's read a lot about spiritualism, visited the Assembly office and museum, and even attended another message circle just yesterday, this time at Forest Temple, a tranquil little outdoor seating area.

Again, she found herself hoping her mother might come through to her, but she was disappointed. This time, it was frustrating to watch one stranger after another get spiritual validation from their lost loved ones through the mediums.

As long as she's here, in the midst of all these people who seem able to talk to the dead—well, she wants to hear from her mother. All morning, she's been toying with the idea of going for a private reading. She can't seem to work up the nerve, though. Not just yet, anyway.

Blue pulls out onto the main road, saying casually, "My house is up around the bend."

"You don't live in Lily Dale?"

"Not inside the gate anymore. We moved to this place last year after my dad had it built."

"This place" turns out to be a neo-Victorian home that is sprawled on a rolling green hill beside the lake. It has cupolas, fishscale shingles, and a gingerbread porch like the houses in the Dale, but it's five or six times their size. No peeling paint or loose shutters here.

Clearly, the Slaytons are a social notch above Odelia and her neighbors. Remembering the resentment in her grandmother's voice when she talked about Blue's father going Hollywood, Calla wonders if she might just be jealous of his high profile, and financial success.

Maybe, but that doesn't seem like Odelia's style.

Calla asked Evangeline the other day why none of the mediums appear to be millionaires if they're psychic. "Don't they know what the stock market is going to do? Can't they just, I don't know, make huge bets in Vegas or something and get rich?"

Evangeline shook her head at that. "It doesn't work that way."

Calla, who has heard that line once too often regarding mediumship, wanted to demand in frustration, "Then how the heck *does* it work?"

But there are some things, she's beginning to realize, that just can't be explained about this place and its people and their gifts.

There are some things you probably can't understand unless you're one of them.

And despite the strange things that have happened to her here, Calla is beginning to feel as though she might just belong in Lily Dale after all.

Which is too bad, because her time here is running out.

About five miles down Route 60, Aldrich's ice cream parlor is busy even in the middle of a weekday afternoon. Calla wouldn't have minded sitting in one of the cozy booths with Blue, but they were all taken, so they sat on stools at the counter. He ordered a Cloud Nine sundae—a brownie buried under ice cream, marshmallow, whipped cream, and fudge. She would have shared it with him, but he didn't ask her, so she ordered one scoop of cinnamon ice cream.

Now, watching him finish the last crumbs of his vanilla-ice-cream-soaked brownie, Calla finds herself telling him that she isn't thrilled to be leaving for California soon to start school.

"Yeah? I'd love to do that. Anything other than one more year at Lily Dale High sounds good to me."

"You go to Lily Dale High?" she asks, surprised. She would have guessed he went to some exclusive school somewhere else.

"For the past two years."

"Where were you before that?"

"At a private school in Buffalo." Ah. So she was dead-on. *It takes one to know one.*

"You didn't like it?" she asks.

"I loved it. They didn't like me." He grins and mimes opening a door and kicking someone out with his foot. "But that's okay. One more year here, and I'm gone."

"One more week here, and I'm gone," she returns. Unlike flirting with Jacy, with Blue it's second nature.

"Or you could stay." His bare leg brushes her bare leg under the counter.

She looks up at him and realizes it was no accident. He's looking at her as if he really, *really* wants her to stay.

"You mean, live with my grandmother and go to school here?" For some reason, that idea doesn't seem as ridiculous as it probably should.

"It's a tiny school. You probably know half the senior class already."

"I doubt that." Though he, Jacy, and Evangeline—oh, and Willow—are among them.

"Well, you said you don't know a soul in California. So you're ahead of the game here."

She tilts her head and smiles at him. She can't help it. "Maybe I'll think about it."

"Want to get together tomorrow night for coffee and tell me your decision?"

He's asking her on another date, she realizes—if you can call this a date. "Sure. Why not?"

As Blue pays the check at the register by the door, she stares absently at several posters taped in the window and wonders why she told him she'd consider staying in Lily Dale. She can't do that. Her father would never let her.

Then again, she never would have expected him to let her come here at all. And it would solve his housing problem. The only affordable, livable place he's found so far, with a good public school, is that place he checked out by the beach—but it turns out it isn't even available until November.

Wait a minute—what if Calla stayed here for a few more months, started school in Lily Dale, then finished in California with Dad? That way, he could stay where he is for now and save money, and they could rent the beach house in November.

Excited about her plan, Calla is about to mention it to Blue. Then she blinks, startled to realize that a familiar face is smiling out from one of the sun-faded posters on the window.

It's the girl she first saw in the garden at Odelia's house that first night, and again, more clearly, the next morning in her

kitchen. And watching the house from the street on yet another night.

Plastered above her photo is the word *MISSING*. Beneath is
a phone number to call with information—1-800-KIDFIND—
along with the details: Kaitlyn Riggs was last seen at a shopping
mall near Columbus over six months ago.

But . . . that doesn't make sense. She was here with her
mother just a few weeks ago.

It's an old poster, Calla tells herself, heart racing. *She must
have been found since then.*

But what about Mrs. Riggs's tearful reaction when Walter
brought up her daughter?

All at once, it hits Calla, so hard she clutches her stomach
as if it were a physical blow.

When they were at Odelia's that night, and again the next
day, Calla never saw the woman even glance in her daughter's
direction, much less speak to her. It was almost as if she didn't
know she was there.

But I saw her, Calla thinks, followed by, *Maybe I'm the only
one who did—or could . . .*

Because she's a ghost.

Lying awake in her bed, Calla almost wishes she hadn't
thrown away the clock. She has no idea what time it is, but it
feels as though she's been tossing restlessly for hours, wondering about Kaitlyn Riggs.

She called the toll-free number that was on the MISSING
poster and found out that the case is still open. Kaitlyn hasn't
been found. When the man who answered asked if she had a

tip to report, she almost blurted out that she'd seen Kaitlyn in Lily Dale, New York. But she couldn't do it. If Kaitlyn were really here, in the flesh, her mother would, of course, have seen her. She couldn't.

So either Kaitlyn is dead, or she has a lookalike sister, an identical twin. There are two ways to find out: call Elaine Riggs—she's listed; Calla called information in Columbus to make sure. Or she can check with Odelia, who will be able to tell Calla whether Mrs. Riggs was here alone or had a companion. A visible one, anyway.

Which is going to sound like one strange question. And might tip off Odelia that she isn't the only one who can see dead people around here.

I'm not ready to admit that to her, Calla thinks. *I'm not even ready to admit it to myself.*

But if Mrs. Riggs's daughter is dead, she deserves to know. For closure. People need that.

As horrific as it was to have Mom die, it would have been far worse if she had just vanished . . . wouldn't it?

Maybe not. If she had vanished, there would still be hope.

Who am I to take away Mrs. Riggs's hope?

Who am I to get involved at all?

Suddenly, there's an explosive slamming sound nearby. Calla gasps and bolts from the bed, clutching herself.

What on earth *was* that? She fumbles for the lamp, terrified. Finding the switch at last, she blinks in the blinding light. It takes a minute for her eyes to adjust, and she feels trapped, heart racing, wondering if she's even alone in the room. At last, she looks frantically around and sees . . .

Nothing.

Not at first, anyway. Everything is as it should be, not a thing out of place or even disturbed.

Except . . .

Oh. The picture.

One of the frames on the dresser has toppled forward. She knows they were all upright earlier because she looked at them all, right before she went to bed. It's become a habit; she's comforted seeing her mother's face, even though she's so young in the photos.

But how could it move? The window is closed. There's no fan, nothing stirring in the room. There's no reason the picture would topple over in the middle of the night. No *earthly* reason.

As she listens to her own breath, coming hard and fast, she begins to sense that she isn't alone in the room right now.

"Are you here?" Calla whispers—to whom, she doesn't know. But someone's here. For some reason, the realization isn't frightening. Unnerving, yes. The skin on the back of her neck is prickling. But there's nothing menacing about whatever—whomever—is here.

"Mom?" she whispers, looking around, hoping to catch a glimpse of . . . someone.

There's nothing. This ghost, if there is one—*and there is*—isn't going to materialize.

"Mom? Are you here? Are you trying to tell me something?"

Her breathing growing more shallow, Calla reaches a trembling hand slowly toward the frame. She knows even before she turns it over which picture it is.

The one at the prom, with the boy Calla thought looked so familiar but never has been able to place.

"Oh, that's Darrin," Ramona says immediately, looking at the framed picture in her sunny kitchen. "Yeah, your mother went out with him for a while. Odelia couldn't stand him."

"Really?" Calla asks, trying not to sound too breathlessly concerned. "Why not?"

"Odelia said he gave off negative energy. She was right. I felt it too. We all did."

"*All* . . . who?"

"A lot of people around town. You know. Darrin was just . . . *trouble.* You could sense that from a mile away. Well, the rest of us could, anyway. But not Stephanie."

"Why not?"

"I don't know. . . . Love is blind?" Ramona offers with a feeble shrug, handing the picture back to Calla. "She just wouldn't give him up. Not even after her mother told her she had to."

It's hard for Calla to imagine laid-back Odelia being that strict.

"Want some Pepsi?" asks Ramona, opening the fridge and peering inside.

"No thanks," Calla says, thinking it's kind of early for Pepsi. So early she's surprised Ramona didn't bat an eye when Calla popped up at the door at this hour—seven thirty—and asked if she had a few minutes. She merely said, "Sure, come on in," and mentioned that Evangeline and Mason were still sleeping. She seemed to sense Calla wanted to speak to her alone.

Ramona pours herself a tall, fizzy glassful, then sits at the table and pulls out a chair, patting it for Calla.

"Where is he now?" Calla asks, sinking into the seat, still clutching the picture.

"Darrin? I don't know. He got into drugs—that happens sometimes around here."

"What do you mean?"

"Some people I've known, especially teenagers, aren't comfortable with their sensitivity. It can be a frightening, isolating feeling to discover that you have an awareness of spirit energy."

Yeah, no kidding.

"Unfortunately, some people tend to self-medicate with drugs or alcohol as a means of escaping what they can't accept." Ramona sounds like she's reciting from a medical journal.

"So what happened to Darrin, exactly?" Calla asks, to keep her on track.

"He was spiraling pretty badly, last I knew. But that was years ago, before he . . ."

"Before he what?" Calla prods impatiently when Ramona trails off. She can't help but be frustrated that she's discovered so little about her mother's forbidden love, whom she still believes she might have seen somewhere before . . . if only she knew where that might have been.

Ramona looks her in the eye. "Before he disappeared."

"He *disappeared*? What do you mean?"

"One day, he just vanished, and nobody ever saw him again."

Calla's jaw drops.

"His parents thought something terrible must have happened to him," Ramona goes on conversationally, turning back to the easel. "So do I, actually. Maybe he was dealing, and not just using, and a deal went bad . . . who knows?"

"Who knows? It seems like *someone* would know," Calla mutters, "with all these psychics around. I mean, isn't that what you people do?"

She's conscious of her phrasing, knows that she's deliberately using *you people* to set herself squarely across the line from Lily Dale's psychic population. She can't help it. She's feeling cranky again. You'd think that all these people with their special powers would know what happened to Mom's old boyfriend—or at least would be able to bring Mom through to Calla.

That's why you're so angry. Admit it. You're frustrated that you're here in a town where supposedly nobody is really dead, and you still can't reach Mom.

"You mean, do people around here have the ability to find missing persons?" Ramona asks, unflustered by Calla's attitude. "Some have done that, sure."

Calla thinks about Kaitlyn Riggs. *Am I really going to pretend I never saw her?*

"I'm sure Darrin's parents tried to find him that way, but for whatever reason, they didn't. It isn't foolproof," Ramona points out.

"Do you think he's dead?"

"Maybe."

"But wouldn't you know? Wouldn't his parents know, if they're mediums?"

"Nothing is more powerful than the bond between a parent and a child." Ramona's hazel eyes bore into Calla's. "There are some things a parent might not want to see, or accept."

She nods, thinking not of Kaitlyn now, but of her own mother. If she hadn't seen Mom with her own eyes, lying there in a pool of blood, she might never have believed she was gone. There was no denial in the face of that evidence, though.

"I should go," she tells Ramona abruptly. "I have . . . stuff to do."

"Sure. But listen, anytime you want to talk about your mom, I'm here. Okay?"

Calla nods, then flees.

Outside, alone, she takes a deep, shuddering breath. Try as she might, she can't block the memory of her mother's corpse from her mind's eye. Nor can she erase her troubling questions about what happened to her.

Accidents might happen to everyone, but Mom falling down a flight of stairs?

Okay, so if it wasn't an accident, what's the alternative?

Calla never allows herself to think past that crazy question, or consider why she alone seems to be wondering about it. The police aren't suspicious. Dad isn't suspicious.

And I'm not, either. I can't be. I won't let myself be.

So why can't she completely accept it, as everyone else did?

I just can't. Especially now that I know I might actually be psychic.

What if her vague, nagging suspicion is intuition, and grounded in reality?

It might mean Mom didn't just die. Somebody killed her.

Again, Calla casts a thoughtful look at the boy in the picture. Darrin.

"Hello?"

Calla is so shocked to hear Kevin's voice that she nearly drops the phone.

She shouldn't be, though. She called his house. He lives there. Why wouldn't he answer the phone? If she had been thinking straight, she might have prepared herself for that possibility.

But she hasn't been thinking straight, upset about her growing misgivings about Mom's so-called accident. She has no proof. Just a hunch. If that's what you call it in Calla's case.

"Is . . . is Lisa there?"

"Calla." He says her name softly. "Hi."

"Is Lisa there?" she repeats, pressing the phone hard to her ear with a trembling hand.

"No. She's out with my mother. What's wrong? Are you okay?"

"No." It comes out as a half sob. "I mean, yes," she says in a small, shaky voice.

"No, you aren't. What's going on?"

"It's just . . . I'm homesick, I guess," she says in a rush. And it's true. Homesick for Kevin, for her mother. For what can never be again. Homesick. And terrified.

"I know how that feels," he says unexpectedly. "I was really homesick last fall, when I first got to Cornell."

"You never told me that," she murmurs.

"Yeah. Well, it didn't last for too long. I got used to the dorm, then I got busy with classes and I started meeting people . . . it got better."

Meeting people. Like Annie.

"Please tell Lisa I called?" she says tightly. "Thanks. Good—"

"Wait . . . guess what? My parents got me this car to take back to school."

"Really?"

"Yeah, they didn't really want to. Mostly because they didn't want me driving from Florida to New York alone."

Maybe you can take Annie with you, she wants to say. Despite everything else she has to worry about, it kills her to think of him driving around with another girl in the passenger's seat.

"Anyway, I'm headed back up there to school the day after tomorrow, so if you need . . . anything . . . I mean, Cornell is only a few hours from you, and . . . like I said, I'll have a car."

"That's good. For you, I mean." *It has nothing to do with me because we're broken up.*

"Yeah. So if you need anything . . . ," he says again.

You'd be the last person I'd call. "Thanks," Calla says, "but I'm really fine. Just tell Lisa to call me when she gets home, if it's not too late."

"It might be. They went to Orlando."

"Well, no big deal. I'll catch up with her later."

She hangs up, shaking, glad her grandmother is down at the café having coffee with her friend Andy. Calla needs some time to pull herself together after hearing Kevin's voice.

If only . . .

No. You can't start wishing for things that can never be.

It's just, talking to Kevin, feeling as needy and alone as she has lately—well, it made her feel like maybe he still cares.

But it's not as if Kevin just asked her to get back together. No, he just told her he can help her if she needs him. Because he's a nice guy. No other reason. He might be only a few hours from here when he gets to school, but he's with someone else now. Annie. So what does it matter?

You need to focus on reality. On what is. Not what if.

And reality is, she has far bigger problems to worry about right now than ex-boyfriends.

FOURTEEN

The lake.

How can Calla stay away from the lake when it's somehow connected to her mother?

I can't. No matter what Odelia says.

Walking along the deserted, grassy shore in the late-afternoon sunlight, she stares into the water and wonders what to do. About her mother. About Kaitlyn. About California.

Nothing, nothing, and nothing, she tells herself grimly.

She has no proof that her mother's death was anything but an accident.

She does know she saw Kaitlyn Riggs or someone who looks just like her here in Lily Dale and that she's still missing, but what is she supposed to do about that?

And she's going to California Labor Day weekend because that's the plan, unless she asks permission to stay. Odelia will agree, she's certain. Her father might, too. But is it what she wants? Just days ago, all she wanted was to leave, and now—

Something catches the corner of her eye. She jerks her head around to see a familiar woman standing several feet away, in the shadows of a huge old maple tree. She has a dark bun, dark eyes, a slight build . . . and she's wearing a *strange, flowing, light-colored dress.*

It's her.

The woman she saw here before, and that day in the cemetery in Florida.

Her hand is outstretched. She's holding something out toward Calla.

Mesmerized, Calla walks closer, forgetting to be startled or afraid.

On the woman's palm is something small and silvery. She lifts it directly under her face so that the item is clearly visible.

It's a charm—the kind you attach to a bracelet. It's etched with the outline of a rugged landscape and some words Calla can't quite read.

She leans closer until she can.

Rock House.

That means nothing to her. Nothing at all. Should it? *Rock House.* She squeezes her eyes closed to think about it, feeling as though she's forgetting something, and comes up blank.

When she opens her eyes again a moment later, the woman is gone.

Was she even here at all? Or am I losing my mind?

Calla exhales shakily and looks up at the wispy clouds

floating across the pale blue sky, as if she can possibly find an answer there. *Nope. You're losing your mind.*

She lowers her head again, and something catches her eye on the ground at her feet.

Bending over, she retrieves the silver charm.

So she really was here. It wasn't Calla's imagination.

Rock House.

"Oh my God," Calla says breathlessly, remembering.

That night at the message circle, Walter said the same thing when he read Elaine Riggs. He saw a rock . . . and a house.

At the time, Calla thought he was seeing two separate images, and maybe he was.

But on this souvenir charm, they're put together: one phrase. The name of a place.

But where is it? And what does it have to do with Kaitlyn Riggs?

"Calla? Is that you?" Odelia calls when Calla walks in the door, as if she's been waiting for her.

"Yeah, it's me." Still clutching the strange silver charm, she heads toward the stairs. She isn't in the mood to talk to her grandmother. She really needs to pull herself together before her coffee date with Blue later. That, or cancel it.

"Wait." Odelia appears in the doorway, wearing a red T-shirt, lavender Bermuda shorts, and flip-flops with a fist-sized plastic flower above the thong. "I have to tell you something."

Calla stops short. "What's wrong?"

"Nothing's wrong. But you missed a phone call, and it was some good news for you."

"Dad's letting me stay?" she blurts. Oops. Of course that's not it. How can it be? She's never even brought that up.

"You want to *stay*?" Odelia asks slowly, looking stunned. "Here in Lily Dale? With me?"

Calla opens her mouth to tell her she doesn't, but somehow, she can't bring herself to say that. Because it isn't true. She *does* want to stay. At least for a while.

"I . . . I don't know. Maybe." She can't look her grandmother in the eye.

Odelia walks over to her and hugs her. Hard. "Well, I would really love that. Having you here has been . . . I don't want to get all mushy on you, so I'll just say it's been good."

Calla nods. No way is she going to get mushy if Odelia's not. "It *has* been good."

"Listen," Odelia says, "you can stay as long as you want. Forever and a day."

"I was thinking maybe just until November. There's a beach house Dad found, and it isn't available till then, so . . . I was thinking I could start school here, then transfer."

"Would you really want to do that?"

Calla shrugs. "Why not? I'm already changing schools from Tampa, anyway. It's not like I'm going to have this great senior year no matter where I am."

"You never know. Here, especially. The high school is small, but it's good. Your mother loved it, back then." Odelia is wearing a wistful, faraway smile.

Calla opens her mouth, wanting to ask about Darrin. But, no, she shouldn't. Not yet.

"So you asked your father about staying?" Odelia asks.

Calla shakes her head. "Can you ask him for me?"

"*Me?* I don't know if that's—"

"Coming from you, he'll take it more seriously," Calla tells her. "You can tell him that I've been doing well here, and that the school is good, and all that stuff."

"Oh, hell, why not? I'll talk to him if you want me to. The sooner the better, if you're serious about staying. I'll have to get you registered at school, and get supplies. . . ." She sounds so enthusiastic, it sounds like a done deal.

Dad will never let me, Calla thinks. Then again, he isn't used to being the decision maker in her life, and Odelia can be very take-charge and persuasive . . . just like Mom was.

"Wait a second." Calla remembers something. "You said I missed a phone call, good news. What is it?"

"Oh! I almost forgot. Your friend Lisa called. She said she's coming to visit."

"*What?* When?"

"Her brother is driving her here—they're leaving first thing in the morning. She'll be here Friday, fly home Monday."

"Are you serious? Lisa's coming here?" *With Kevin?*

"She asked me if it was all right with me, and of course I told her it is. I just hope it's all right with you."

"Yes!" Then, hardly daring to breathe, Calla asks, "Is . . . is her brother staying, too?"

"No, he's dropping her off, then heading to school. Cornell, right? He must be smart."

"He is." *But not smart enough to hang on to me,* Calla can't help thinking. "Do you mind if I use the phone to call Lisa?"

"Not at all," Odelia says, "but first let me use it to call your father. I don't want to waste another minute."

"When you're done checking your e-mail, want to hang out for a while?" Evangeline asks twenty minutes later, watching Calla pull the desk chair closer to the keyboard.

"For a couple of minutes," Calla murmurs, dragging the mouse and clicking on the Internet icon. "I . . . have to be someplace in a little while, though."

"Really? Hot date?"

Calla looks up sharply. "Who told you?"

"Oh my God! You really have a hot date? With who, Blue Slayton?"

"How did you know?"

"Wait, I was just kidding . . . so you do? With *Blue*?" When Calla nods, she shrieks. "I can't believe it! I *so* knew he was into you! Tell me everything!"

"Just . . . give me a minute online, okay? Then I'll tell you. Not that there's much to tell."

"There must be something juicy if you're going out with Blue."

Calla shrugs and flashes Evangeline a distracted smile, hoping she's not going to stand there in the doorway the whole time and watch her use the computer.

Good. She's not. Evangeline returns the smile, then goes into the next room, where the television is on. She's alone; her aunt took Mason to Applebee's and a movie down in Fredonia.

Waiting for the search engine screen to pop up, Calla thinks again about the whirlwind of action at Odelia's house just now. First came Odelia's report that her father is actually going to consider letting her stay. On the heels of that was Calla's giddy conversation with Lisa.

Calla can hardly believe she'll be here in Lily Dale by the weekend. She said her parents are probably letting her come only because they don't want Kevin driving all that way alone, and neither of them can take off work to accompany him.

"But who cares why?" she crowed. "I get to come see you. Isn't it great?"

Calla has been trying not to picture Kevin slowing his new car in front of Odelia's house just long enough for Lisa to jump out. Of course *he's* not coming here to see her. Lisa is. He's just the chauffeur.

And she's not going to give him another moment's thought.

Definitely not right now, anyway, because the search engine is up and she's typing the words *Rock House* in quotes.

A list of links pop up a moment later. She clicks on the first one, reads a few lines, and gasps.

Rock House is a real place, all right.

It's a cave in Hocking Hills State Park, just outside Columbus, Ohio.

Having coffee with Blue Slayton is the last thing Calla feels like doing, but it's definitely too late to back out.

Calla knows, because she tried. But when she called Blue's house, the housekeeper told her he wasn't home.

She's lying, Calla thought. Somehow, she sensed that Blue was home but didn't want to talk to her. Or maybe not to anyone. Whatever. She couldn't demand that he get on the phone so she could break their date, and it wouldn't be polite to leave him a message saying she can't go.

No, the girl who was dumped in a text message would never let anyone down in such an impersonal manner.

She finds herself checking her reflection in the living-room mirror one last time as she hears a car door slam, then footsteps coming up the porch steps, through the screen.

"You look pretty," Odelia says from her recliner, where she's reading *People* magazine with her bare feet up, flip-flops kicked into a distant corner.

"Thanks." Calla notices that her eyes in the mirror, accented by makeup for the first time in ages, look too huge in her thinner-than-usual face. A generous layer of concealer couldn't mask the circles beneath them, either.

Other than that, though, she looks fine. Maybe even pretty. She's wearing jeans and a snug-fitting black tank top with spaghetti straps, and she's left her hair down to fall around her bare shoulders. Not that she's trying to impress Blue Slayton or anything.

"Have fun," Odelia says from her chair as the bell rings and Calla heads for the door.

"Yeah, I will."

Blue—whose eyes, jeans, and chambray shirt reflect his name—smiles appreciatively when he sees her, jangling keys in his hand. "Ready?"

Not really. She should be having a heart-to-heart talk with Odelia about Kaitlyn Riggs and Rock House Cave in Ohio.

But that will open the door to a whole lot of something Calla isn't ready to face.

"Ready," she tells Blue, who's waiting.

As she follows him out the door, she pats her back pocket to make sure she can feel the outline of her cell phone there. In case she decides to put Plan B into motion.

Ten miles northwest of Lily Dale, Route 60 ends at the shore of another lake, this one much bigger than Cassadaga. The grayish green water looks like the ocean, stretching all the way to the horizon. But Calla knows her geography well enough to realize that the Atlantic is a good four hundred or five hundred miles from here, on the opposite end of New York State.

No, this is one of the Great Lakes—Lake Erie. They're in Dunkirk, a small city of tree-shaded neighborhoods lined with two-story clapboard houses, brick schools, plentiful church steeples, nineteenth-century storefronts, and a couple of factories. After Lily Dale, it feels like a metropolis. They passed a Super Wal-Mart on the way into town, and Calla asked Blue to stop there on the way back so that she can pick up a few things.

He wrinkled his nose. "You don't want to shop there."

She does . . . but she tells him to forget it. Maybe she can get Odelia to take her someday.

The municipal parking lot isn't at all crowded at this hour on a weeknight, but it takes Blue a few minutes to find a suitable space for his BMW, one that's a good distance from the café, where there aren't cars parked on either side.

"Sorry we have to be way out here." He opens Calla's door for her. "I got a door nick on this a few weeks after my dad gave it to me, and he wasn't thrilled."

She finds herself wondering about his dad as they walk toward the store, but she doesn't want to ask. He hasn't mentioned him except in passing, and he hasn't brought up his mother at all. Probably because she isn't a part of his life. Was she ever?

Calla finds herself feeling empathetic—or maybe it's more sympathetic—for him. He comes across as self-assured on the surface, but she suspects there's a vulnerable little boy somewhere beneath.

The Chadwick Bay Café is a stone's throw from the long, wide pier jutting into the lake. Fishing boats and tugs are moored alongside it, and there's a flock of ducks on the sloped launch at the base of the pier. A family is there—father, mother, little girl—doling out a loaf of bread to the ducks and laughing as they fend off swooping, angry gulls.

Seeing them, Calla feels an ache in her throat and quickly turns away.

"If they're not careful, they're going to end up covered in seagull crap." Blue seems utterly uncharmed by the scene. But Calla sees a fleeting glint in his eyes, and she realizes that he, too, might long to be part of a family like that again. If he ever was.

Death, even divorce, is one thing, but . . .

How could his mother willingly leave him? Calla tries to imagine how she'd feel if her mother had abandoned her by choice. It's all she can do not to reach for Blue's hand and give it a squeeze as he opens the door to the café for her.

The place is cozy, just a counter and a couple of small round tables with matching wrought-iron chairs. A glass case holds baked goods that seem picked over at this hour, and there are several stainless steel pump carafes behind the counter, along with an espresso machine.

The teenage girl wiping down the counter looks up. "Hey, Blue, hey, Wil—oh."

Not *Willow*, exactly, but that's what she was about to say.

Blue must be a regular here with his ex-girlfriend. Nice.

"This is Calla," Blue announces, as Calla looks everywhere but at the counter girl, and him. "Calla, this is Sue."

They both say hi. Calla makes an effort to smile and show the girl that she can fit in here every bit as well as Willow . . . who, come to think of it, didn't strike her as friendly at all.

"What do you want?" Blue asks her.

"Just . . . coffee." She never drinks the stuff, but maybe it's time she started. A little jolt of caffeine might be just what she needs. *That, or a solid night's sleep,* she thinks grimly.

"Flavored, or non?" Sue asks. "We have hazelnut, Viennese Cinnamon, Irish Cream, Black Forest."

Calla, who was hoping for chocolate, says, "I'll just take nonflavored, thanks."

Blue asks for a complicated beverage in what sounds like a foreign language. The girl pours Calla a steaming cup from the carafe marked Regular before foaming the milk for Blue's drink. Calla adds a liberal amount of half-and-half and two packets of sugar to her cup, takes a sip, and makes a face.

"What's wrong? Too hot?"

She looks up to see Blue watching her. "No, it's just . . . it seems kind of . . . flavored."

"Let's see." He takes the cup and tastes it. "Yeah. Hey, Sue, you gave her Irish Cream."

"I did?" The girl looks up, surprised. "Are you sure?"

"Positive. Here."

Sue takes the cup from him, sniffs it, then looks at the carafes. "I could swear I took it from the Regular."

"You did," Calla tells her. "I saw you."

Frowning, Sue takes a tiny paper cup, fills it from the spout of the Regular, and sniffs it.

"This isn't flavored," she says, and hands it across the counter. "See?"

Calla sniffs it warily. She's right. It doesn't smell like Irish Cream at all.

"I guess I took the other cup from the wrong carafe by accident," Sue says with an apologetic shrug. "It's been a long day. Sorry."

As she gets Calla another cup—this time, regular—Calla uneasily studies the row of carafes. The flavors are clearly marked on laminated signs. The Irish Cream one is toward the end, a few carafes away from the Regular one. It's not as if they're right next to each other and Calla simply *thought* Sue was filling her cup from the Regular carafe when in fact it was the Irish Cream one.

No, she knows what she saw.

Yet she also knows what she tasted. That was definitely Irish Cream. Even Blue agreed.

"Here you go. Sorry about that, again." Sue hands her the fresh cup and turns back to preparing the espresso drink.

Calla fixes the new cup with half-and-half and a couple of sugars. Then she takes a cautious sip.

This time, it's regular. But a chill slips down her spine.

She realizes there suddenly seems to be a chill in the café as well.

And in the air, mingling with the aroma of brewing coffee, is the unmistakable fragrance of flowers.

"Hello, is this Mrs. Riggs?"

"Yes . . . who is this?"

Standing in the shadows on the pier outside the café, Calla hesitates, clenching her cell phone hard against her ear. "I . . . I'm a friend. I might have some information about your daughter."

There's a gasp on the other end of the line. "Who is this? Are you calling from . . . Florida?"

Caller ID, Calla realizes with a sinking heart.

Well, of course. Mrs. Riggs can trace the call to Calla's phone. And she'll have the police do it, too. She might even think Calla had something to do with her daughter's disappearance.

Oh, God. What am I doing?

She should have stopped to think this through, but she didn't. She had come up with the plan earlier, somewhere between the Taggarts' house and Odelia's. Still, she wasn't even sure she was going to go through with it.

She was sitting there trying to sip her coffee and listen while Blue talked, but she was still unnerved by what had just happened. It wasn't anything overtly scary, but the mistaken coffee, the chill, the scent in the air—it was all just *off*.

She needed to get out of there . . . and yes, she needed to do something about Kaitlyn. So she impulsively snuck a hand into her back pocket and pressed the ringer button on her cell phone to make Blue think she had a call. Then she pulled it out, answered it, and excused herself to take it outside. Blue didn't seem to mind. He was chatting with Sue the counter girl again before Calla even made it to the door. Still, she has to make this fast, because he might come out here looking for her.

"I'm only trying to help you, Mrs. Riggs," she says in a rush, keeping one eye on the café door. "Please . . . you have to believe me. I'm—I met you in Lily Dale."

Silence.

"You came to see my grandmother, Odelia Lauder, for a reading. And—and you heard from your father in the auditorium here the other night. A man named Walter brought him through for you. And he was showing you a rock, and a house. Do you remember?"

"Ye-es." The word is so soft Calla can barely hear it.

"Mrs. Riggs, I think I can help you find Kaitlyn."

"How?"

"Because—" Calla's breath catches in her throat.

"Because I'm a psychic," she admits quietly. *Finally.* "Like my grandmother. Do you . . . have you ever heard of Hocking Hills State Park?"

Blue insists on walking her up to Odelia's front door, even though Calla tells him it's not necessary.

She just wants to be alone with her thoughts right now.

Elaine Riggs did know where Hocking Hills State Park is, and she flatly told Calla that it was miles from where Kaitlyn was last seen.

"Still, I think you should ask the police to search there," Calla told her, and the woman hung up pretty quickly, without saying whether she would take that advice or not.

There's nothing else Calla can do. It's out of her hands. She tried.

"Watch your step." Blue slips a hand beneath her elbow as they walk up to the porch. "It's dark out here."

It is. Odelia must have forgotten to turn on the porch light. She does that about as often as she forgets to lock the door. Or maybe it was just as deliberate tonight, to set the stage for romance with Blue?

"Hey, listen, Calla, I'm sorry about what happened back there."

His comment takes her by surprise. What is he talking about? Can he possibly know about her call to Mrs. Riggs?

Maybe. He's psychic, remember?

"What do you mean?" she asks cautiously.

"I mean at the café. When Sue called you Willow, when we first came in. She's my ex-girlfriend."

"Sue?"

He laughs. "God, no. Willow York. That's who Sue was talking about. People are kind of used to us being together, so . . ."

"Now you're not together?"

"Nope."

"Because it's no big deal if you—"

Blue presses his index finger against her lips and says in a whisper, "Shh. Stop talking."

"Why?"

"Because if your lips are moving, I can't do this."

Gently grasping her upper arms with his warm hands, he leans in, eyes closed. His kiss is expert: long, but not wet or sloppy. *It's like a movie kiss,* Calla finds herself thinking as he pulls back.

"So . . . I'll call you," Blue says cheerfully, and then he's gone, leaving her alone in the dark, heart pounding and knees weak.

FIFTEEN

That dream . . .

Again.

The fragmented one about the lake, Mom, Odelia. It's haunted Calla the last two nights again, jarring her out of sleep. She has no way of knowing what time she's waking up, but it's definitely been in the wee hours. Like, say, around 3:17 a.m.

The last two days have pretty much been an exhausting blur.

The recurring dream and Kaitlyn Riggs aren't all that have been haunting Calla.

Blue Slayton's good-night kiss at Odelia's front door was pretty . . . memorable. Oh, yeah. Definitely. He told her he'd call her, but he hasn't yet. And she wants him to. Yes, he's got a little more swagger than she'd like, but what girl wouldn't be drawn to Blue Slayton? Especially after that kiss?

Now it's Friday, noon, and since he hasn't called yet, she

doesn't expect him to until at least Monday. He mentioned that he's flying to Manhattan for the weekend with his father, who's going to be doing some television appearances there.

Lisa will be here in just a few hours, though. Calla can't decide whether she should tell her about everything that's been going on here or keep it to herself. Not the Blue Slayton part—that, she'll tell Lisa . . . and hope it gets back to Kevin. But the rest? The stuff about the ghosts, psychic mediums— and Calla being one of them?

Maybe not. Lisa is her best friend. But there's a good chance she won't understand.

A good chance? Ha.

She can't possibly understand. A few weeks ago, Calla herself thought Lily Dale—and everyone in it—was absurd.

Now she's a part of it. How insane is that? She's part of it, and Lisa—and Kevin, and Dad—is not. Funny that she suddenly feels as though she has more in common with people like Odelia, Evangeline, even Blue, than with people she's known—and loved—her whole life.

But Mom was part of Lily Dale, too, once.

No, Mom still is. Calla can feel her here. *And she's trying to get through to me—I know she is. If I stay, she eventually will. Sooner or later.*

That's why her hand is shaking so badly as she dials the phone at precisely twelve o'clock, with Odelia hovering over her shoulder. Dad called yesterday and said he was going to sleep on it for one more night and have a decision for her by nine his time, before he leaves to teach his first class.

"Is it ringing?" Odelia asks, and Calla nods, holding her breath.

Dad picks up after two rings. "Hi, honey."

"Hi, Dad." Her voice comes out kind of strangled-sounding.

"Did you sleep well?"

Geez, talk about a loaded question. Calla tells him that she did, and wishes he would get on with it, but he starts telling her about the weather there this morning. That it's beautiful and warm and there's not a hint of smog.

"What's it doing there?" he asks.

"Raining." As usual. Calla thought Florida was bad in summer, but there, it storms briefly almost every afternoon, then clears. In Lily Dale, it's pretty gray much of the time.

"That's too bad," Dad says. "Your mom always said the weather wasn't great up there."

Is he trying to convince Calla that she doesn't want to stay?

No. He isn't. Because he takes a deep breath and says, "Listen, honey, if you want to stay until November . . . you can."

Suddenly, there's a lump in her throat and tears have sprung to her eyes.

Looking at her, Odelia shakes her head glumly and whispers, "He said no, huh?"

"No," Calla whispers back, "he said yes."

So why is she suddenly feeling so torn?

Because I miss my father. A lot more than I even realized until right now.

"Thanks, Dad." She tries to sound more enthusiastic than she suddenly feels.

"And listen," he says, "I'm going to fly there to visit just as soon as I can get things squared away here, and find a decent airfare. I can't go that long without seeing you."

"That sounds good." Yes, she misses him. But she can't

help hoping that there won't be a decent airfare for a while, because the second he finds out she's living in a spiritualist colony, it's all over for her here.

From her perch on Odelia's porch, Calla can't see whether the approaching red Toyota has Florida plates, nor can she see the driver and passenger. But she knows, without a doubt, that it's Kevin and Lisa. She could feel them getting closer long before the car appeared, and her foot has been jiggling a loose floorboard in nervous anticipation for the past ten minutes.

The moment the car pulls up at the curb, the passenger's side door opens and Lisa pops out. "Calla! Oh my God, I can't believe I'm here!"

Calla can't quite grasp it, either, even when Lisa is on the porch grabbing her, hugging her. It feels so good to see a familiar face from home that Calla forgets to look for Kevin. But only for a moment. Then her gaze shifts over Lisa's shoulder, and she sees him, taking two big suitcases out of the trunk.

He looks good. So good. His hair is longer again, streaked blond from the sun, and he's tan, of course. He's wearing flipflops, long surfer shorts, an untucked, half-buttoned madras shirt, and a familiar necklace made of hemp and puka shells. Familiar because Calla bought it for him, one day when they were out at Pass-a-Grille. She recognizes it even from here.

He sets the bags on the ground, then looks up. His eyes instantly collide with Calla's, and his face lights up.

So does hers. She can feel it. And she can't help it. She'd give anything, in this moment, to walk down there and throw herself into Kevin's arms.

213

Somehow, though, she doesn't. She just smiles at him, and he smiles back.

"Can you bring those up, Kev?" Lisa calls, and he already is.

Calla sees him glance up at the shingle above Odelia's porch as he lugs the suitcases up the steps. He frowns but says nothing, just deposits the bags on the porch with a grunt.

"Man, those are heavy."

"You're staying, too?" Calla asks, then realizes he might think she doesn't want him to. And she does. Desperately. "I mean, I'm really glad. I just . . . I thought you had to drive back to school tonight."

"I do. These are Lisa's bags."

Oh. Her face grows hot. She should have known. And she shouldn't have hoped.

"I think she packed everything she owns," Kevin adds.

"Not everything. I forgot hair gel. I need to get some right away. I've gone two days without it because *he* wouldn't go out of his way to get it, and every time we stopped we were in the middle of nowhere."

"I hate to say it," Calla speaks up, "but you still are."

"What do you mean?"

"I mean there's a Wal-Mart ten miles away, and that's about it for shopping as far as I can tell."

"Then let's go right now."

"Now?"

"Look at me!" Lisa lifts a hank of her silky blond hair in disgust.

"You look great," Calla tells her. "And I'll get my grandmother to take us tomorrow. She's, um, busy for the rest of the day." Right. Doing back-to-back readings with clients

214

anxious to get in before the season ends. But Calla isn't about to get into that yet. Not with Kevin here, especially.

Lisa wails and turns to her brother. "You've got to take us to Wal-Mart."

"Me! I've got to drive to Ithaca."

"Please take us to Wal-Mart first, Kev. Come on. I let you keep the AC on high for two days even though I was freezing, and I didn't complain once about your choice of music."

"Sure you did. Constantly."

Calla can't help but grin at that. Lisa likes only country.

"Please, Kev?" Lisa asks. "Come on. It won't take long. I promise."

He sighs. "Okay. Come on, let's go. But you have to make it quick. I need to get on the road to school."

And Annie, Calla thinks grimly, thinking she shouldn't even tag along to Wal-Mart.

But she does. Old habits die hard.

Lisa does most of the talking on the way to Wal-Mart, sitting in the back but leaning forward between the two seats. Even with her there, even in a new car, Calla can't help but feel wrongly comfortable sitting there beside Kevin in the front. If only . . .

No. Stop.

Wal-Mart's parking lot is crowded. As Kevin squeezes his new car into the first available space, Calla thinks, for the first time in a while, of Blue. Blue and his BMW, parked way out where no other car can touch it.

In the store's entryway, Lisa promptly grabs a cart.

215

"Uh . . . how much are you planning to buy?" Kevin asks warily.

"Just a few things."

"Oh, God. I can't watch this."

"Then don't. I'll meet you guys up front in half an hour." Lisa sails away.

Calla looks helplessly at Kevin, who shrugs and sighs. "Looks like we've got some time to browse."

We? So, he's going to stick with her?

Suspecting Lisa did this on purpose, Calla wishes she hadn't. She wants to tell Lisa there's no hope for her and Kevin; he has a new girlfriend now, and she . . .

Well, she doesn't have a new boyfriend, though Blue said he'd call. And when she ran into Jacy yesterday at the library, they talked for over half an hour. She left feeling as though she wouldn't mind seeing him again. Maybe Evangeline will get over him and move on to someone new. If that happened, there would be no reason not to—

"Do you need to get anything specific here?" Kevin asks Calla, breaking into her thoughts. "Should I get a cart?"

"God, no."

There's plenty that Calla needs, though. She picks things up here and there as she and Kevin walk along. Nail polish and remover and emery boards, a couple of books, and—after a slight hesitation—a new digital alarm clock. In the jewelry department, she buys a cheap watch.

"I forgot all my jewelry back home," she feels compelled to explain.

"Right," he says a little sadly, and she realizes he thinks she stopped wearing the Movado because they broke up. She wants to tell him that's not true, but then decides to let him think it is. Let him feel bad that he fell for another girl and dumped her in a text message.

That thought is enough to make her deliberately pause to browse the clearance aisle on their way to the front register, even though she can feel him getting antsy.

"There's some good stuff here," she comments, picking up a packet of stationery emblazoned with a C. If she can't e-mail anyone, she'll have to keep sending real letters.

"So, are you all set, then? Lisa should be ready," he adds, checking his own watch. It's new, Calla notices. A gift from Annie? *Grrrrr* . . .

She can't resist saying, "Just give me another minute to make sure I'm not missing any bargains . . . oh, look at those cute Santa cups!"

Reaching toward the shelf that holds out-of-season holiday items, she suddenly stops short, feeling a blast of cold.

The air-conditioned store was hardly warm to begin with, but all at once, it's absolutely arctic. Shivering, noting the uneasiness that whooshed through her along with the chill, Calla asks Kevin, "Do you feel that?"

"What, the AC? I guess someone just cranked it. Brr."

As she looks up at him, she sees a woman standing beside him. The woman from the cemetery, and the lake. She stares into Calla's eyes.

"What? What do you want?" she blurts out, and Kevin jerks his head around to look behind him, then back again at Calla.

"Who are you talking to?"

The woman is still standing right there, still staring, though Kevin doesn't even see her.

She's trying to tell me something.

Who are you? she asks silently, not daring to speak out loud in front of Kevin again.

Aiyana. The word—a name—pops into her head as clearly as if the woman had spoken it.

Maybe she did.

Aiyana? Is that your name? Another silent question . . . but somehow, the woman is reading Calla's thoughts.

She responds with a pleased nod. Aiyana.

"Calla?" Kevin touches her arm.

As he speaks, the woman begins to morph before her eyes, going from sharply focused to blurred, like a photograph taken when the object was in motion.

"No . . . wait!" But the figure has gone quickly transparent.

And finally, she isn't there at all.

She's gone. Yet the chill still lingers over Calla. Shivering, she raises her arms to hug herself. As she does, she hears something start to wobble on the shelf beside her.

I didn't even brush against it, Calla thinks incredulously, startled when a moment later whatever it is falls to the floor and shatters.

Looking down in bewilderment, she realizes that she's surrounded by shards of green glass. Dismayed she looks back at the shelf. "How did that happen?" The broken object was one of the holiday items near the Santa cups: cute green shamrock-shaped candy dishes.

"Careful," Kevin says, as a store employee approaches.

"Don't get cut on the glass, Calla." He touches her arm to pull her back from the broken shards.

"I'll pay for it," Calla offers, jittery not just from the inexplicable accident, but from Kevin's warm hand on her bare skin.

"Not necessary," the employee, a manager, says with a shrug. "These are marked down to, like, a quarter each. We've been trying to unload them since Saint Patrick's Day."

"I know, but still—"

"Really, it's fine," he says, and calls someone to come to the clearance aisle for cleanup.

Rattled, Calla can only apologize again, profusely, before following Kevin to the register, where Lisa is waiting with a full cart. Kevin uses his parents' credit card to pay for everything in it, and everything Calla has as well.

"It's no big deal," he tells her as they head out to the parking lot with their bags.

It is a big deal, to her. But not nearly as disturbing as what happened back in the store.

Aiyana, Calla thinks, over and over again as they drive home. *Aiyana*.

By Monday afternoon, Calla is more than ready to see Lisa off to the airport.

Which is interesting, because on the other hand, it was hard to watch Kevin drive away on Friday night. He gave her a quick hug before he left, similar to the one he gave his sister. But the brief contact made Calla wistful all over again.

"Remember," he said, "if you need me, I'm not far away."

"I know. Thanks."

She's had a good weekend with Lisa, overall. It's been nice to have some company, and to think about something other than spirits for a change. And yes, she'll miss Lisa when she's gone. It's just that her friend has disdain for everything and everyone in Lily Dale. That was obvious from the moment they got back from Wal-Mart and she spotted Odelia's shingle for the first time. Of course, she was polite to Calla's grandmother, who couldn't be a more gracious hostess. But whenever Odelia was out of earshot, Lisa talked about her as if she's a batty old woman.

Which is exactly what I thought she was, too, before I got to know her, Calla reminds herself uncomfortably, as she watches Lisa give her blond hair a final pat and set her brush on the bureau.

Calla removed all Mom's old pictures before Lisa got here. In part because she doesn't really want to share them with anyone, and in part because she was afraid of another ghostly middle-of-the-night incident. Lisa has been sharing her room, sleeping in Mom's old bed while Calla sleeps on a cot Odelia borrowed from Andy.

Calla hasn't set up her new digital clock yet, worried that it, too, might trigger something supernatural. Then again, she was having the dream even after she got rid of the old clock, and she hasn't had it since Lisa got here.

"I just have to put on some lotion," Lisa tells her, checking her reflection again in the mirror. "My skin gets so dry when I fly."

Calla rolls her eyes and watches Lisa rummage through her crowded toiletries bag. She pulls out a tube and squirts some lotion onto her palm.

As she rubs it into her skin, Calla sniffs, realizing the room is filling with a hauntingly familiar scent. There's no telltale chill in the air this time, but the floral perfume is unmistakable.

"What? You don't like it either?"

Startled, Calla looks up to see Lisa watching her. "What?"

"This smell. It's too strong, right?"

"You . . . can smell it too?"

"Smell what? My lotion?"

Her *lotion*? It's her lotion that smells? Sniffing the tube Lisa thrusts under her nose, Calla realizes that this time, the floral scent has a perfectly ordinary source. No wonder there's no chill.

" I just bought it the other night at Wal-Mart because they didn't have the honeysuckle one I usually like," Lisa goes on, closing the tube.

"What scent is this?"

"I don't know." Lisa turns it over, looks at the label, and reads, "Lily of the Valley."

As Odelia steers the car up Cottage Row again that night, Calla feels numb with exhaustion. All she wants to do is fall at last into her own bed—Mom's old bed—and sleep.

They saw Lisa off at the airport, but her plane left three hours late because of Florida thunderstorms. It's raining here, too. Thunder rumbles and lightning bolts light the sky over the lake as Odelia parks in front of the house and turns off the headlights. Rain patters hard on the roof of the car.

"We'll have to make a run for it when it lets up a little," she says, fishing around under the seat. "Unless I find an umbrella in here."

Calla doubts she will—though you never know. Odelia's car is as cluttered as her house, and Calla's mind right now.

But she doesn't want to think about any of it—Aiyana, lilies of the valley, even Mom. Not tonight, anyway, even now that Lisa's gone.

She looks longingly toward the house as another bolt of lightning zaps the sky, illuminating the world for a split second.

In that second, Calla sees that there's a figure on Odelia's porch. Human, but is it alive or dead? Her heart beats a little faster as she gazes at the ominous shadow, which appears to be wearing some kind of hooded cloak.

"Come on," Odelia says, abruptly opening the door. "It's letting up."

Calla hesitates.

"Let's go!" Odelia commands, and she's off, splashing her way through the rain to the door.

Calla follows reluctantly, realizing as she bolts toward the house that Odelia can see the person on the porch as well, because she appears to be talking to him or her. Which doesn't necessarily mean it's not a ghost, of course.

As she mounts the steps two at a time, she can see that the person isn't wearing a hooded cloak, it's a raincoat. And it's not a ghost—it's a real live woman. A woman Calla recognizes.

"Calla," Odelia says, "Mrs. Riggs would like to speak to you."

Odelia isn't happy. That much is obvious. Her unhappiness has nothing to do with the fact that she's sitting in her recliner like a drowned rat, probably cold and uncomfortable.

No, it has everything to do with Calla, also cold and uncomfortable and drowned-rat-like.

Calla's sitting on the couch next to Elaine Riggs, who turned down Odelia's offer of hot tea and said she has something important to say, then is heading back to the White Inn down in Fredonia, where she's spending the night. Apparently, she spent at least a few hours on Odelia's wet porch, waiting for them.

Before she says whatever it is she has to say to Calla, though, she's found it necessary to tell Odelia what led up to this impromptu visit.

So . . . now Odelia knows.

That Calla saw the ghost of Kaitlyn Riggs. And that she called the girl's mother to tell her to search a remote park based on information she received from a spirit.

And Odelia doesn't like this, any of it. Not one bit. Which doesn't surprise Calla, because obviously Mrs. Riggs is here to complain to Odelia that her granddaughter has been meddling where she doesn't belong.

"The reason I'm here," Elaine Riggs says at last, her voice trembling a little, "is to thank you."

"To thank me?" Calla echoes, startled. "For what?"

"For finding Kaitlyn."

The rain has subsided into a steady drip from the drainpipe above the porch by the time Calla finds herself out there again. In silence, she and her grandmother watch Elaine Riggs climb into her car and drive away.

Calla doesn't dare turn her head to look at Odelia. She can feel her grandmother's anger—and is bewildered by it.

True, Mrs. Riggs's story doesn't have a happy ending.

But at least it has an ending. Closure. Thanks to Calla.

Kaitlyn Riggs's strangled body was found yesterday morning in the woods not far from Rock House Cave in Hocking Hills State Park. The police still don't know what happened to her, but they think she was abducted from the mall parking lot by a stranger. They even asked that Calla be brought in to speak with them, to see if she has any impressions of Kaitlyn's killer.

She doesn't. And when she looked questioningly at Odelia, her grandmother somewhat stiffly told Mrs. Riggs she wasn't sure she was comfortable with Calla doing that. "We'll let you know," she said, "after we've discussed it."

Which Calla isn't particularly eager to do.

"Let's go in," Odelia says now. "It's cold out here. And we have to talk."

"Can we talk tomorrow?" Calla asks, eager, once again, for bed. "Please . . . I'm so exhausted."

Odelia hesitates. "We can. But there's something I want to say to you first. Right now."

"What is it?"

To Calla's surprise, Odelia grabs hold of her shoulders and leans in to look closely at her. "This is important, okay? You obviously have a gift. And you chose not to tell me . . . for whatever reason. Which I respect. You don't have to confide in me . . . about most things. But now that you're here, you're over your head in something you don't fully understand. Something that might even be dangerous."

Calla swallows hard. "Dangerous . . . how?"

"Kaitlyn Riggs was murdered, Calla. And you were given information about her case. The way you chose to share it with her mother . . . well, I know your intentions were good, but I wish you'd come to me first. It takes years to learn how to deal sensitively with people who are grieving. Sometimes it's still hard for me, and I've been at this forever. But what I'm most concerned about is that you could have gotten yourself hurt."

"How?"

"Kaitlyn's killer is still out there somewhere."

Calla nods slowly as a chill slithers down her spine. "Okay. I get it."

"We'll talk more tomorrow," Odelia says, giving her a squeeze. "And do me a favor . . . don't mention this to anyone, okay? You haven't . . . have you?"

"No. Not a soul."

"Good." Odelia smiles. "It's going to be okay. I promise. You just . . . have a lot to learn. But you're in the right place. And it's a good thing you're staying. I hope you haven't changed your mind."

Calla hesitates. Has she?

"No," she says at last, feeling as though a wall has come down between them. "I haven't changed my mind, Gammy."

Odelia smiles.

A few hours later, Calla wakes from a fitful sleep. It's happening again, God help her.

The only way we'll learn the truth is to dredge the lake.

She refuses to open her eyes, trying desperately to slip back into unconsciousness. Maybe if she could just finish the dream. . . .

But it's useless. There's nothing to do but open her eyes, knowing what she'll see on the face of the brand-new clock, which she plugged in and set before climbing into bed earlier. She also pulled all the picture frames out of the drawer, eager to have her room back to normal and to get a good night's sleep.

So much for that.

Sure enough, the florescent digits of the clock—green, this time, instead of red—read 3:17.

Come on. Did you really think buying a new clock was going to change anything?

Her mind flits back to what happened in Wal-Mart the other day.

Aiyana. The strange woman only she could see, who seemed to be trying to tell her something just before . . .

Just before . . .

With a gasp, Calla sits straight up in bed and looks again at the clock's glowing green digits. *Green.* 3:17.

That's a time of day, yes. But it can also be . . . a date.

3-17. Green. Saint Patrick's Day.

And—oh! The Irish Cream coffee. The shamrock dish she broke in the store. None of that was an accident. It was all tied to . . .

Saint Patrick's Day. But *why*?

Even as she wonders, tinkling music fills the room.

She listens for a moment before realizing that it's coming

from the music box on her nightstand. That doesn't make sense, but it must be, because she recognizes the melody.

Reaching for the bedside lamp, she flicks it on and blinks, momentarily blinded.

It takes her a moment to grow accustomed to the light. When she does, she sees that the jewelry box is wide open, and the song—why is it so familiar?—is coming from it.

How can it be open?

She distinctly remembers tucking her new Wal-Mart watch inside it earlier, when she found it in the bag that still held the clock. She latched the top of the jewelry box securely.

Now a series of other memories begin to slam into her, each more forceful than the last.

Bam!

Saint Patrick's Day . . .

Mom baking Irish soda bread.

Bam!

Doorbell rings. Calla answers it. Mom's coworker is there. The one she saw at the funeral. Todd, or Tom. That's it. His name was Tom. He had a manila envelope under his arm, she recalls, the memory suddenly as vivid as if it were a movie playing before her eyes.

Tom looks nervous, but he seems as though he's trying not to act it. Yeah, he's whistling when she opens the door. He asks for Mom, then leans against the door frame and starts whistling again as Calla goes to find her.

Bam!

The tune he's whistling is the same one spilling from the music box right now, and . . .

Bam!

"Oh my God." Calla leaps from the bed and rushes toward the dresser, snatching up the frame she showed Ramona. There's no mistaking it.

Tom's face is an older version of the one in the photograph on her dresser.

Bam!

Tom is Darrin.

How can that be? Stunned, still clutching the frame, Calla realizes that the music is growing louder. She turns slowly back to the music box. Rather than winding down, its melody is somehow increasing in tempo and volume.

Calla throws the frame onto the bed and moves toward the little jewelry box, her hands pressed over her ears as the music grows almost deafening.

Leaning over the box, she realizes that the watch she placed there earlier isn't readily visible, as it should be. Instead, lying on top of the other jewelry in the box is a familiar object.

An emerald bracelet, caked in dried mud.

AUTHOR'S NOTE

The spiritualist community of Lily Dale, New York, is a real place. Of course, I've fictionalized all of the characters in my book, as well as some community elements—for instance, there is no Lily Dale High School—and I've taken some creative liberties with other details. But the town itself is pretty much as I have described it: a quaint, isolated, gated Victorian community of ramshackle nineteenth-century homes clustered along the grassy shore of a picturesque country lake. Its residents are primarily spiritualists, some of whom are registered mediums and/or healers who advertise their calling on painted shingles hung above their doors.

I grew up a stone's throw away in Dunkirk, the small city on Lake Erie visited by Calla and Blue in this book. As teenagers, my friends and I frequently made the ten-minute drive during the summer "season" to Lily Dale, eager to consult with the psychic mediums who lived within its old-world iron gates. Unlike many visitors, we weren't necessarily trying to get in touch with the dearly departed. No, back then, we were mainly concerned about our futures—and our love lives.

That said, I was definitely spooked whenever a spirit would pop up with a message for me—especially when the eerie messages made sense. How, I wondered, could a stranger possibly have known about any of that? I'd scribble notes during some sessions and run the identifying details by my parents and grandparents later. They often recognized the ghostly relatives who came through, even when I didn't. Of course, they did their best to remain skeptical—especially my dad, whose motto in life is "I don't believe it unless I see it." Even he eventually got some spine-tingling evidence that there might just be something to the Lily Dale experience.

Very little has changed in "the Dale" over the past twenty-odd years since my first visit. The Victorian cottages are still ramshackle, the suggested "donation" per reading hasn't inflated much, and the official season remains restricted to July and August, though some mediums are in residence year-round. Now that I'm an adult living the "future" I was once so curious about, I still find myself drawn to Lily Dale.

If you are too, you can check out the community's official Web site at www.lilydaleassembly.com.

A PSYCHIC CHAT

WENDY CORSI STAUB *was thrilled to have the opportunity to chat with Dr. Lauren Thibodeau, a registered medium in Lily Dale, New York. Dr. Thibodeau has been a registered medium with the Lily Dale Assembly since 1996.*

WCS: Dr. Lauren, at what age, and how, did you first realize you were . . . is "gifted" the right word?

LT: I first showed signs of strong psychic ability as soon as I was able to speak, so about age two or so. My grandmother helped me by explaining that not everyone could see or hear what I could, but that I could always come to her with questions. Lucky Calla, though she might not feel that way all the time. I know it helped me to have an older person's support and help, though.

WCS: It's interesting that it was your grandmother who guided you, just as Calla's grandmother helps her in the Lily Dale book series. I just finished reading *When Ghosts Speak* by Mary Ann Winkowski, and her grandmother did the same. Is this ability frequently handed down through older females in a family?

LT: I believe it's like any other talent that runs in families. Musical talent, artistic talent, athletic talent, mechanical talent—lots of talents have a genetic component. This one is no different in that sense. And like any talent, developing it takes devotion and time.

WCS: My Sicilian grandma "sees" people who have passed, more frequently now that she's approaching ninety, and now I and other females in my family have begun to sense we may be similarly gifted. I'll also share that Grandma is a devout Catholic and doesn't particularly like to discuss this "talent."

LT: I have heard that kind of story often. And surprisingly, quite a number of modern Spiritualists have Catholic backgrounds. In fact, we have three former nuns and a couple of former priests living in Lily

Dale. It tends to be a "female thing" much of the time. There is research suggesting that strong intuition is related to brain structure—that the two hemispheres, right and left, have more connecting nerve fibers in women. That means we are able to move between the creative right brain and the logical left brain more easily.

WCS: Does that explain, in part, why there are more female than male registered mediums in Lily Dale? I've always wondered about that!

LT: I think women are also more tuned in to relationships, generally speaking. We often hear it called "women's intuition" and, although it may come more naturally to women, men certainly have it too.

WCS: Do male mediums work differently, then? Focus on different types of readings, perhaps, or in different areas of psychic work?

LT: It tends to follow your interest patterns and your life experience. If you are a man interested in cars, much of the information the spirit world sends would follow that. You might find you "get cars" a lot. As in, "I have a man here, he shows me a 1967 Buick . . ." to start off the identification process.

WCS: Can you describe how you receive psychic impressions? How do you see (or hear or speak with) people who have passed?

LT: You are presented with impressions—that's the right word. Everyone has what I call an "intuitive style." It might be very visual, or very auditory, or very sensory or body-based, sort of a gut feeling. Over time these blend together and you reach what I call the "knowing zone," where you just . . . know. Your impressions are also what I call "symbolic shorthand." You learn how to interpret that information through practice, and of course by paying attention. Keeping a record of your own symbols is wise. For example, I get months of the year by flowers. August is a gladiola; March is a crocus.

But this is a two-way street. Some spirit people are better communicators than others, just as some human beings are better communicators than others. That's why you often find that a newly crossed-over person receives assistance from someone who died long before, to help them "learn the ropes," you might say.

WCS: In my research I came across this symbolic shorthand repeatedly. Interestingly, flowers and floral scents play a major role in my Lily Dale books as Calla connects with spirits. So, are the spirits of our loved ones with us 24-7 or do they touch in and out?

LT: When we invite them into our lives, they're more likely to stop by—just like with our friends and relatives here. So it's a touch-in-and-out process. Invitation and openness help immensely. Ask for them, keep them near, in your mind and heart.

WCS: Ask for them aloud?

LT: Yes, if that's your style.

WCS: Or do they "hear" our thoughts?

LT: They do indeed "hear" our thoughts. So if you don't like talking to your long-lost loved ones aloud, reaching out mentally is fine.

While you were gathering information for your books, did you ever ask any mediums in Lily Dale for their help?

WCS: As part of the research process, I've had readings with a number of mediums there over the past several years, though I never mentioned that I was writing a book. Several of them picked up on that, though. When I did approach the Assembly office at Lily Dale, I was warmly welcomed and officially put in touch with Donna Riegel. She graciously answered all my questions, did an incredibly accurate (and emotionally moving) reading for me, then invited me to sit in on her beginning mediumship class that evening.

When you were young and just developing your abilities, were you ever frightened or wary, as Calla is, of your experiences or of spirits?

LT: Mostly I was more frightened of the reaction of adults! The spirits never once bothered me in that way. It's when I would say something adults knew I had no knowledge of that the trouble started. The "how did you know that?!" reaction. In fact, my kindergarten report card had an Outstanding mark in imagination and another for storytelling— only it wasn't my imagination and I wasn't telling stories. Like a lot of naturally talented young mediums I was only reporting my experiences.

WCS: Meaning you were in touch with "imaginary friends" who were actually spirits?

LT: Yes, my imaginary friends were spirits. Children between the ages of three and five in particular have such experiences. For some children, though, it persists. In those cases, it's possible that the child is indeed connecting with spiritual energy and has a sensitivity that is just extended beyond the usual realm. Not really a "sixth sense" but extended sensory perception in general.

WCS: What advice would you give a teenager who may feel that he or she has intuitive abilities?

LT: First, don't panic. Second, start keeping a record or journal— privately. This isn't something you write to post on MySpace or Facebook. Record your dreams. Impressions. What comes to you. What you immediately connect it with. Also make quiet time—meditate or sit alone quietly, regularly.
   Then, start practicing with fairly immediate feedback situations to "fine-tune" things. Tune in to what you think your best friend is going to wear on Friday, but do it on a Tuesday. Write it down. Then see if you're correct. Stand before the door you think will open in a bank of elevators. That kind of thing. This builds your sensitivity.

WCS: You had mentioned that you teach people to "safely" communicate. Would you elaborate on this, since the whole thing is a little scary for someone who isn't accustomed to the idea?

LT: I am a big believer in what I call Declaration. This is self-empowerment. Boundary-setting. For example, "I am not open to spirit communication unless it is positive for me and others" or "I will not have my sleep disturbed" or "I accept only what is in my highest and best interest to know." Just as you might set boundaries in a personal relationship with a friend, you do so with the spirit world.

WCS: Do spirits frequently visit us in our sleep? I've been reading about that phenomenon.

LT: Yes, they often come in our sleep. That's because we're most relaxed then. So in addition to record keeping, it's smart to take meditation time or quiet time, even if it's for only five minutes a day. Then you find that you experience the spirit energies and communications while you're awake, and you sleep better. Now, if you have a truly powerful unforgettable "dream"—the kind in which you can remember every detail weeks, months, or even years later— that's possibly an actual spirit visitation that happened during sleep. Those are rare compared to regular dreams but unforgettable if you've had one.

WCS: I find that comforting! It's happened to me and to my siblings and husband and father. My father, sister, and I all had dreams about my mom, not long after she had passed, and in all of them she was wearing red (we found this out after the fact and the coincidence struck us!). Do you think there's some kind of symbolism or meaning there? We all strongly felt these were visitations and not just "dreams."

LT: When you have that sort of "collective" experience with matching details, you can be assured it's a visitation. And colors often are part of the message.

WCS: I want my readers to know that Lily Dale is a real place. They can visit www.lilydaleassembly.com for more info about it. Dr. Lauren, you're there during the summer "season," correct?

LT: Yes, I'm one of forty or so registered mediums. Have you spent much time in Lily Dale yourself?

WCS: I've been visiting Lily Dale many times a year for as long as I can remember—I grew up a few miles away and return to my hometown every couple of months to visit my family, who all remain in the area. I often make my way to the Dale, not just for research or spiritual healing, but because it's a beautiful, serene setting in any season.

LT: What is your most vivid memory of Lily Dale?

WCS: It was the last place I visited with my mom before she passed away in May 2005. She was in her early sixties and dying of breast cancer, and I had sadly been called home. My father, husband, two little boys, and I took her to her final radiation treatment, then went for a drive because she couldn't bear to return home yet. It was a cold spring day, and we were all crammed into my father's car, driving through the streets of Lily Dale. I realized she and I were thinking the same thing, which remained unspoken because the kids were with us—that after she passed, I could return to Lily Dale and find her. That is exactly what happened. She was in a coma two days later, and she passed away the week following our last visit to Lily Dale. The famous psychic James Van Praagh vividly brought her through to me and several family members three months later, in August, in the Lily Dale auditorium at his workshop.

LT: I'm so glad you had such a meaningful experience at one of our events. If you visit the Dale in the summer, you're likely to find me out and about at one of the daily message services—so say "Hi!" if you visit. I look forward to meeting friends and fans of Wendy—and Calla.

Dr. Lauren is also the author of *Natural-Born Intuition: How to Awaken and Develop Your Inner Wisdom* and *Natural-Born Soulmates: Follow Your Inner Wisdom to Lasting Love.* To find out more about Dr. Lauren or Wendy, visit their Web sites at www.DrLauren.com and www.wendycorsistaub.com.

TRUTH IS INDEED STRANGER THAN FICTION IN THE TOWN OF LILY DALE . . .

- Lily Dale is 60 miles south of Buffalo, New York.

- Founded in 1879, Lily Dale is the largest Spiritualist community in the United States and possibly the world.

- It costs $10 per person to enter the wrought-iron gates of the community during its summer season.

- Several houses in Lily Dale are said to contain energy vortexes, and supposedly there is a spot in the forest that is so charged, the hair on your arms will stand up straight.

- Psychics hang up shingles outside their homes advertising their specialties.

- Inspiration Stump is Lily Dale's holiest place, where the mediums gather daily during the season to give readings to the town's guests.

- Mae West was a Lily Dale believer, and she said that her favorite medium there came to visit her right after his death.

- Harry Houdini, a foe to Spiritualism, so frightened the community that when he came to town, they all locked their doors and hid.

- Lily Dale was one of the first towns to get electricity, and it was originally called the City of Light.

- Susan B. Anthony was a frequent visitor to Lily Dale. Most of Lily Dale's leading psychics over the years have been female, and the women's rights movement had many supporters there.

- Lily Dale psychics rarely have insights about themselves or those people close to them—mainly because they have their own lessons to learn here on Earth, or so they believe.

NATIONAL BESTSELLING AUTHOR

WENDY CORSI STAUB

LILY DALE
BELIEVING

The corridor smells of hot food as Calla makes her way toward the cafeteria after social studies, her fourth-period class.

So far, so good. Things are going better than she expected, being the new kid for the first time since kindergarten. Wait, kindergarten doesn't even count, because everyone else is new too.

Here, everyone else gives off the comfortable, easygoing attitude that comes with familiar territory.

This was familiar territory for Mom by the time she started her senior year here. Just knowing that this is where her mother went to school gave Calla chills when she first walked up the broad stone front steps.

Not *you're about to see a ghost* chills. More like *if you're not careful, you're going to burst out crying in front of everyone* chills.

Calla quickly discovered that beyond the old-fashioned redbrick exterior of Lily Dale High are equally old-fashioned green chalkboards, banks of gray metal lockers, scuffed hardwood floors, and straight rows of desks.

This place is a world away from Shoreside Day School back in Tampa, with its state-of-the-art labs, indoor-outdoor classrooms, and lecture halls housed in a sprawling cluster of sleek, modern buildings that feel more like a college campus than a high school.

Here, she's found her way to every classroom with little trouble—not all that hard, considering that the two-story school has simple L-shaped hallways on both floors. She's been assigned a homeroom and a locker, memorized her combination, and accumulated a stack of textbooks. She's even seen a few familiar faces: Lena Hoffman, who works at the Lily Dale Café, has the locker next to Calla's, and Willow York, of all people, has turned up in most of her classes so far.

When they found themselves sitting across the aisle from each other in health class first thing this morning, Willow acknowledged Calla with a brief smile, which totally caught her off guard.

Not that she expected Willow to stick out her tongue, but still. As Blue Slayton's barely ex-girlfriend, Willow can't be thrilled that he's gone out with someone else. And Evangeline told Calla that Willow knows all about that. "Lily Dale is smaller than any small town you'll ever see," Evangeline said cheerfully. "Everyone knows everything about everyone."

Right. And sometimes even before it happens.

Well, Willow has class, Calla has decided. She's not going to make a big deal out of Calla seeing Blue. Good for her.

And even better for me.

Pausing in the doorway of the cafeteria, Calla lingers to read the posted menu. Sloppy Joes today, like Evangeline predicted.

She reads the menu intently, checking to see what's on it for the next few days. Then next week.

Then, when she can't stall any longer, she forces herself to walk into the cafeteria.

This is what she's been dreading all day: the prospect of eating alone. Unfortunately her one friend, Evangeline, isn't here. When they compared schedules in the hall after homeroom, they found that their paths cross only once a day: in gym.

As Calla crosses the threshold into the cafeteria, her heart sinks. Instead of the small round tables that fill the cafeteria back at Shoreside, there are long rectangular tables. Most of them are filled with people who have known each other since kindergarten. It's going to be impossible for her to duck over to a secluded table alone and hide.

Is lunch even mandatory here? She definitely isn't hungry, thanks to Odelia force-feeding her mush and bacon. She's about to flee when she hears someone call her name.

Looking up, she sees Blue Slayton beckoning from a table filled with guys.

Hmm. Maybe she'll stick around. She walks over, tossing her head a little to get her hair out of her face without being obvious.

"How's it going?" Blue asks when she arrives at his side.

"Great," she says, noticing that he's wearing a long-sleeved jersey in a deep indigo shade that matches his eyes—and his name.

He wears that color a lot, she's noticed, and she's sure it's no accident. He has to be aware of the striking impact. And his clothes are expensive. She can tell by the cotton fabric that looks as thick and soft as his light brown hair, which he might wear in a wavy and slightly unkempt style, but she knows that's no ten-dollar barbershop haircut.

No, everything about Blue Slayton is expertly and deliberately pulled together. The result is effortless good looks that take her breath away a little every time she sees him up close.

"So you haven't gotten lost yet?" he asks Calla, fork poised above a tray that holds two of everything: two sloppy joe plate lunches, two bottles of juice, two ice cream bars.

"Not yet." She wonders if he's going to eat all that himself, or if he's planning to share with someone else. Willow, maybe?

"The only way to get lost around here is trying to find your way home if a blizzard blows in during the day," comments the red-haired, freckled guy sitting next to Blue.

"Yeah, but that only happens, like, once a week in the winter, and so far, we've lost less than a dozen kids that way," Blue says dryly, and everyone laughs.

He introduces Calla to the redhead—Jeremy—and to the other four guys, two of whom are named Ryan. They're all on the school soccer team together.

"Calla's living over in the Dale with her grandmother," Blue tells them, and a couple of them ask her politely about where she's from and how she likes it here.

As she answers their questions, she wishes Blue would invite her to sit down, but he doesn't.

Well, that's probably because he's with all these guys.

Or maybe it's because he's no longer interested in you.

"Hey, Calla," he says abruptly, "want to go out Friday night?"

Or maybe he is interested.

"Sure," she hears herself say as her heart trips over itself. "That would be great."

"Good. I'll call you." Blue drains what's left of his open juice and crushes the plastic bottle in his fist before reaching for the second one.

She takes that as her cue to leave.

But Blue Slayton asking her out again is enough to ease the humiliation, five minutes later, of roaming the room with a full tray, looking for a seat that has empty chairs around it. She doesn't want to just go and plop herself down next to anyone. That would feel kind of . . . bold.

But none of the open chairs has a buffer zone around it, and she can feel people looking up at her as she passes their tables.

She just has to sit down somewhere. Anywhere.

She looks around and her gaze falls on a striking girl with long black hair, porcelain skin, and a familiar face. Willow York again, and she glances up from a conversation she's having with the girl next to her. "Oh, hi."

"Hi." Calla hesitates, still holding her tray.

"Want to sit with us?" asks the other girl, who is African American, with a short, chic haircut, gorgeous dark eyes, and a mouthful of braces. She points to the empty chair across from her and Willow.

"Definitely." Calla gratefully puts her tray on the table and slips into the chair without stopping to see if Willow seems to want her there.

"This is Sarita," Willow says, in a friendly enough tone, "and you and I have already met. A few times, right? But I'm Willow . . . in case you forgot."

She didn't forget.

"Do you live in Lily Dale?" Sarita asks.

"Yeah, I'm staying with my grandmother." Calla decides not to tell her it's only temporary. Why complicate the conversation? "How about you?"

"I live down the road in Cassadaga."

Does the fact that Sarita lives outside the Dale mean she can't see dead people or have psychic visions or premonitions?

What about Willow? She lives in the Dale. Is she a medium?

Even more important: did Willow see Calla talking to Blue a few minutes ago? Probably not. She's acting pretty friendly.

Or maybe she's over him.

Nah. Remembering Blue's piercing eyes—and those broad shoulders beneath the soft cotton jersey—Calla can't help but think it would take any girl a long time to get over him.

Including you, she warns herself. *So don't go letting yourself get hooked on him.*

Yeah. One broken heart per year is more than enough.

Hearing a commotion, she looks over to see that someone just tripped and dropped his lunch tray. Her first thought: *Thank God that didn't happen to me.*

Her next: *That poor kid.*

He's enormously obese, with jet black hair, thick glasses, and a line of fuzz on his upper lip.

A few kids are laughing as, flustered, he wipes red sauce off his hands and starts to pick up the mess.

"Oh, no, poor Donald." Willow is instantly up and out of her seat, hurrying toward him.

"That's Donald Reamer," Sarita comments to Calla. "He's the kind of guy who . . . well, you know. Things are hard for him."

Calla nods. She does know. There was a Donald Reamer at her school in Florida, too—only it was a girl, and her name was Tangie Alvin.

Surprised at Willow's compassion, she watches her hand him a pile of napkins before stooping to salvage what's edible from his dropped lunch. She can see that a group of girls at a table next to them are snickering and rolling their eyes.

After a cafeteria aide has appeared with a mop and bucket and Donald has lumbered on his way, Willow goes over to the table of girls and says something to them. Their smirks vanish and they immediately look uncomfortable.

Willow returns to the table and reclaims her chair without comment. Sarita seems to be taking the whole thing in stride, saying only, "I hope they give him another lunch without charging him."

"Me, too. So . . . what'd you think of Kiley?" Willow asks Calla conversationally, and bites into an apple. Calla notices her tray contains only that, a small container of yogurt, and a bottle of water. Sarita's holds the same.

"Kiley?" For a second, she's blank. Then, "Oh! You mean the health teacher? She seemed nice."

Willow and Sarita exchange a look.

"Yeah, she puts up a good front . . . on the first day. They all do. Just wait. Have you had math yet?"

"It's last period."

"Then you probably have Bombeck, with Willow. He's famous for being hard-core," Sarita says. "My sister was straight A's until she landed in his class. She still talks about him, and she graduated four years ago. My mom even had him and said he was really hard even back then. He's been here forever."

"Well, hopefully I'll be okay." Calla picks up her fork, trying not to wonder whether her own mom might have had Bombeck, and whether she went to school with Sarita's mom. "I usually do pretty well in math."

Straight A's, actually. She's been an honor-roll student all the way through high school, but she doesn't mention that. She doesn't want to sound like she's bragging.

"Math is my strongest subject," Willow tells her. "And even I'm worried. You don't know Bombeck."

"I'm so glad I didn't get him for math," Sarita says contentedly.

"So you have Davidson, right? And who do you have for English?" Willow asks.

As Sarita pulls her schedule out of her backpack to compare it to Willow's, Calla toys with her fork. She's reluctant to dig into her steaming, hearty sloppy joe lunch in front of the other girls. She should have gotten fruit, yogurt, and water, like they did. She wants to fit in.

Then again . . .

Mom was always telling her not to follow the crowd. *Who cares what the other girls are eating?* her mother's voice asks in her head. *Who cares what they think of you?*

I kind of do, Mom. Just this once. Calla closes her eyes, barely aware of Sarita and Willow, who are chatting about a mutual friend. *I can't help it, Mom. I want to fit in here because . . . well, I don't fit in anywhere else anymore.*

Don't worry, you will, her mother's voice says, and she can hear it so clearly in her head that she wonders if her mother is actually here.

Focus. Maybe if you really focus, you'll be able to see her.

She tunes out all the background noise, thinking about her mother. About how desperately she misses her.

Please. Please, Mom. If you're here, let me see you. Please.

Gradually, Calla becomes aware of a strong presence. Someone is watching her. She can feel it.

She braces herself, opens her eyes, and looks up, expecting to see a shadow or even her mother's ghost. Or . . . Kaitlyn's.

Please let it be Mom this time. Please . . .

WENDY CORSI STAUB grew up in New York, just a few miles from the real town of Lily Dale. As a teenager, she and her friends visited the mediums there, hoping to find out whom they would marry. One medium told Wendy that her future husband's name would begin with the letters M-A. She wrote down the medium's prediction and forgot about it until years later, when she found her notes from that reading. By then she was married to her husband, Mark.

Wendy has published more than sixty books for adults and teenagers and is a *New York Times* bestselling author of several suspense novels. She lives in Westchester, New York, with her husband and their two sons.

Visit her Web sites at
www.wendycorsistaub.com
www.myspace.com/lilydalebooks
www.myspace.com/wendytheauthor